VICKY

BY CATHERINE STORR

✵

Marianne and Mark (*Faber Fanfare*)
Rufus (*Faber Fanfare*)

for younger children

✵

Clever Polly and the Stupid Wolf
Tales of Polly and the Hungry Wolf
Kate and the Island
Puss and Cat
Robin
The Story of the Terrible Scar

The Painter and the Fish
with pictures by Alan Howard

VICKY

Catherine Storr

FABER AND FABER
London �֍ Boston

*First published in 1981
by Faber and Faber Limited
3 Queen Square, London WC1N 3AU
Printed in Great Britain by
Redwood Burn Ltd, Trowbridge*

British Library Cataloguing in Publication Data

Storr, Catherine
  Vicky
  I. Title
  823'.914[J]   PZ7

ISBN 0–571–11762–7

For
Marghanita Howard

1

"Mum'd have been pleased," Chris said, when the last guest, full of ham and cake, port or sherry, had left.

"You mean, there being such a lot of people?"

"Who wanted to come. Who liked her."

"People did." Vicky couldn't imagine anyone not liking her Mum, who in her turn had liked most people, had been kind about those she'd not liked. She'd been warm, ready at the least excuse, to befriend. As Vicky had most reason to know. If Mrs. Stanford hadn't been that sort of woman, Vicky might well have spent all her sixteen years in a Children's Home. Because her own young mother, in the next bed to Mrs. Stanford in the maternity ward, had died when Vicky was two days old, leaving nothing to point to her identity but a name, which probably wasn't her own, and a small suitcase of the clothes in which she'd meant to carry her baby away. To where? No one knew. The usual exhaustive enquiries had to be made, the police, the social services, the Salvation Army all called in to try to trace relatives, but every attempt met with blank failure. So eventually Mrs. Stanford, who'd been mothering Vicky, as well as her own Chris, while they were still in hospital, was allowed to take home two baby girls, first fostering, then adopting the one who wasn't actually her own. Vicky and Chris had been brought up as sisters, twins. Now their Mum had done the first selfish thing they could remember. Going off like that, without a word of warning.

"There's pounds of ham left. And cut bread and butter.

1

What'll we do with it all?" Vicky asked.

"The ham can go in the fridge."

"What about the bread and butter?"

"We could make it into sandwiches and toast them," Chris said.

"There's too much. We couldn't ever . . ."

"There's a whole jug of coffee. I suppose we could keep that for tomorrow. And that enormous pot Mrs. Chalmers lent us, full of tea no one drank. Put it down the toilet, Vicky."

"And we've got more than half of one of the cakes. That won't keep. They all tasted stale, anyway."

They looked at each other, standing in the front room which hadn't often been used in their mother's lifetime. The kitchen had been the centre of family life. There Mrs. Stanford had cooked and washed and ironed, and there she had listened, through innumerable cups of tea, to their troubles, their confidences and their conversation. This front room was as strange and empty as the occasion.

Chris suddenly left the room. She came back with a large black plastic bin liner in her hand. She swept the slices of anaemic cake into it, and followed them with the cut bread and butter, lying neatly dove-tailed on the pink leaves of sliced ham. Vicky looked on in amazement.

"Chris! What're you going to do with all that?"

"I want to get it out. Everything." Her hand hovered over the main chunk of the tinned ham.

"Why don't you leave that? Dad likes it. And anyway . . ."

"I'll get rid of this, though," Chris said. She emptied two bottles of sweet brown sherry down the kitchen sink. One was half, the other three-quarters full. "Horrible stuff. I can't think why anyone drinks it."

"We could have used it for cooking," Vicky said.

"Who could? I don't cook with sherry. Dad wouldn't touch it if I did," Chris said. She picked up the plastic bag and went to the back door. Vicky heard the rattle of the dustbin lid in the yard. Chris came back, her hands empty.

"I wanted everything out," she said.

2

"But . . . someone could have had it."

"Who? How're we going to find them? Anyway, I don't want to have to bother. We've got to get it all straight and finished with. Everything to do with . . . with funerals. That's how Mum would have liked it."

"All right. Let's wash up, then. Will you? Or shall I?"

"Don't mind. One of us'll have to dry, though, so as to get the good china back into the cupboard."

In the end it was Chris who washed and Vicky who dried the delicate plates with a pattern of roses, embellished with golden stems and leaves. Vicky didn't think she'd ever seen this china being used. It had been kept in the glass-fronted case in the front room; once a year Mum had taken it out and washed every single piece. Chris and Vicky had only just grown old enough last year to be allowed to help. "But I'll have it out for your weddings," Mrs. Stanford had said. But she hadn't had the chance. They had had it out for her funeral. Vicky sniffed.

"Don't. You'll start me," Chris said.

"It's the china. Thinking how she used to say . . ."

"I know. But we had to have it out for today, didn't we? She'd have wanted us to. Like for a party. A serious party. To say goodbye."

They washed and dried in silence. Such a lot of plates and cups and saucers. So many knives and forks and glasses. So many people had wanted to come to say their goodbyes.

"Where's Dad?" Vicky asked presently.

"I think he's back in the front room."

"What's he doing?"

"Don't know. He went out for a *Standard*," Chris said.

"A *Standard*? But it's . . ."

"No, it isn't. It's Wednesday." They were both startled to find that a day that had felt so different from all other days could produce anything as ordinary as a weekday paper.

There was another silence. Chris handled the china carefully. Vicky took a third tea towel, hanging two others, soaking, up to dry.

"Nearly finished," she said.

3

"There's still the teapot. The rosy one." It was not round like ordinary pots, but oblong, with squared shoulders. The lid was topped by a knob in the shape of a rose, delicately moulded, each petal standing just separate from the others. As a child, Vicky had thought it the most beautiful thing she'd ever seen. Receiving it from the hot soapy water, she patted it dry and remembered her Mum saying, "It's a beautiful pourer, too," and demonstrating this, on one of those annual cleansings, sending a stream of clear hot water from the elegant little spout. It was thinking that Mum wouldn't ever again enjoy pouring out of that spout that upset Vicky. Little unexpected things like that.

"Dad might like a cup of tea," Chris said.

"I'll ask him, shall I?"

"I'll put the kettle on. I could do with one anyway."

Vicky went to the door of the front room. Mr. Stanford had the paper spread out, but he was not reading it. He was sitting, looking at nothing, his eyes fixed. He did not turn when Vicky opened the door.

"Dad? We're having tea. Want a cup?"

He did turn then and looked at her. He said, "Yes. A cup'd be nice. Thanks."

"Here? Or in the kitchen?"

"I'll come through. In a minute," he said, not moving.

Vicky went to the kitchen. Chris had made the tea in the old everyday brown pot. She poured three cups and was generous with milk and sugar.

"Funny how tea makes you feel better," Vicky said burning her throat just pleasurably.

"It's a stimulant. Tannin. Paul says," Chris said.

"Paul was at the church this morning."

"He came back here for a bit," Chris said.

"Why didn't he stay?"

"Too many people, he said."

"Stephen was there too. At the church, I mean."

"But he didn't come here?"

"I didn't see him," Vicky said.

"I didn't either."

There was a pause.

4

"Is Paul coming round here tonight?" Vicky asked.

"Expect so. He didn't say he wouldn't."

"Chris?"

"What?"

"Are you and him going out together? Serious, I mean?"

Chris took a loud sip of tea before she answered.

"I don't know," she said at last.

"Hasn't he. . . ? I mean, hasn't he said anything?"

"Not like you mean."

"It's been more than a year," Vicky said.

"That's not very long."

"You like him. A lot. Don't you?"

"I've always liked him," Chris said.

Vicky looked at her. Chris was just as she always was. A bit swollen round the eyes, perhaps, but it hardly showed. As pretty as ever. If anything she'd got better-looking as she grew up. Other girls got lumpy or spotty or awkward. Not Chris. She remained neatly made, with good features, lovely skin and hair, and an astonishing composure which didn't often desert her.

Mr. Stanford came into the room. He looked at Chris and Vicky without altering his expression, then sat down in the third chair. Chris poured his tea, and Vicky added the milk. He took a long swill. The kitchen was unusually quiet. Ordinarily at this time of the evening there would have been at least one conversation going on, and very likely the radio or the telly as well. Vicky wanted to say something to break the silence, but she couldn't think of anything that would sound right.

It was Chris who asked, "What're you going to do tonight, Dad?"

"There's a meeting. But I don't know that I'll go. . . ."

"Why not?" Chris asked.

Mr. Stanford hesitated. "I'm not sure."

"Mum wouldn't have minded. She'd want us to go on doing whatever we were going to. You know she would," Chris said.

"She would. It's just I'm not sure I want to go," Mr. Stanford said.

5

"What sort of meeting?" Chris was practical.

"Electing a delegate to conference."

"Important?"

Mr. Stanford turned on her. "'Course it's important. Don't you ever read anything in the paper except for who's murdered someone, or about the Queen and that? Don't you know what's happening in this country today?"

Chris said peaceably, "Sometimes I do. Not like you, though."

"Well. You're only young. You'll learn." He said, to show that peace had been offered and accepted, "Good cuppa tea."

"Want anything to eat, Dad?" Vicky asked.

"Couldn't."

He looked round the kitchen, acknowledging the difference from the litter of an hour before.

"What you done with all that food?"

"Threw it out. Except for the ham," Chris said.

"Threw it out?" For a moment Vicky thought he was going to reproach them with the starving millions in the Third World. He'd done that when they'd been kids and hadn't finished their plates. But Mum had always been there to remove the plates and to promise that the leavings wouldn't be wasted. What she really had done with them, Vicky didn't know. She didn't think she'd ever seen them again.

Mr. Stanford sighed. He said, "Suppose that's right."

Chris took the opportunity to say, "Dad! About Mum's things. . . ."

"What things?" Sharpish.

"Clothes. Shoes." But that was only the beginning. Hairbrushes, powder compacts. Beads, a brooch or two. Bottles of patent medicines, her sewing basket, a long box of knitting needles, lavender bags so old they'd lost all their scent, books, bits cut out of papers, old picture postcards . . . Chris couldn't begin to list all the things that made up the cheerful clutter which had surrounded her Mum.

"Clothes. Get them out. Unless there's anything you want. No. Get the whole lot out," Mr. Stanford said.

6

"Everything. As well as just clothes?"

"You can leave the dresser drawer."

One of the three drawers in the kitchen dresser held a characteristic jumble of things Mrs. Stanford had needed in her everyday life, and forgotten treasures. Her purse with the housekeeping money, her Post Office book. Her National Insurance card, the television licence, a certificate for excellence in drawing, forty years old. In a small cardboard box, held together by an elastic band, was a large garnet brooch which had belonged to Mrs. Stanford's grandmother. Huge and hideous. She'd never worn it.

Presently Mr. Stanford left for his meeting. Vicky and Chris drank more tea, sitting in front of the television, hardly taking in what was happening on the screen. It's like, Vicky thought, as if we had to have something, going on, a noise or people doing ordinary things, not taking any notice of us and how we're feeling. Like putting sticking plaster on a cut finger. It doesn't stop it hurting, it just prevents it getting rubbed or broken open and made worse. For minutes at a time you could almost forget what had happened. Then you move, it throbs, and the pain starts up again.

Paul came round. More tea. He sat with them for half an hour, talking perhaps more than usual, and all about matter of fact things. His course at college, friends they all knew, a book he'd lent Chris. He talked about their Mum too, but in an ordinary voice, not hushed or embarrassed. As if she happened not to be in the room. But he spoke of her in the past tense; he wasn't pretending that any minute she might come in.

It was ten o'clock when he left.

"I'm going to bed. I'm ..." Vicky had nearly said, "dead".

"I'll come too."

"I feel as if today had gone on for ever," Vicky said.

"That's how I feel."

They lay flat, exhausted, in the beds they'd had since they came out of drop-sided cots. Vicky had thought that this was when she'd cry, but no tears came, there wasn't even a

7

lump in her throat. She was too tired to feel anything but aching fatigue and a longing to be unconscious, not to have to think.

Out of the darkness Chris spoke.

"Vicky? You awake?"

"Mm."

"I just wanted to say . . ."

"What?"

"About Paul. And me."

"You said he hadn't said anything."

"He hasn't. But. I think we probably will get married. Not yet. Not for ages. But we shall."

"How d'you know? If he's never said?"

"He doesn't need to say. I know. And he knows I know."

Vicky's immediate reaction was, shamefully, "Then I'll be really alone." Of course she couldn't say it. She said, instead, "You'll be happy." And Chris answered, "It isn't that. Not being sure we'll be happy. It's just that we couldn't, either of us, be with anyone else."

After she was sure Chris was safely asleep, Vicky did cry. Silently. Selfishly. For what she had lost and for what she was going to lose.

2

It was nearly a month later, on a Sunday, when Vicky came downstairs from two hours of hard work, cleaning the bedrooms, the bathroom and the upstairs passages. She and Chris shared the housework, and this Sunday it had been her turn to try to catch up with the dust that seemed to come from nowhere. She found Mr. Stanford in the kitchen, sitting at the table which was covered with papers, envelopes, boxes; a clutter of *things*.

"What on earth . . .?"

"I'm going through that drawer."

There was a rectangle of emptiness between the other two white painted drawers. The third stood empty, on end, beside Mr. Stanford's chair. He had obviously turned it upside down on the table, and was now bewildered by the hotch-potch in front of him.

"Tea?" said Vicky, making for the kettle.

"I don't mind."

Vicky loooked at him out of the corners of her eyes as she filled the pot. He looked miserable. No wonder. She wanted to go over and put her arms round him as she'd done when she was little, as Chris would have done now. She wanted to offer to help, but she didn't know how. Although he'd been kind, even loving, although he'd tried not to make any difference between the way he treated her and Chris, Vicky had known for the last few years that he didn't feel the same about them. Unlike Mum, who had hugged and spoiled, spanked when necessary, sometimes

9

snapped, always seemed to love them both equally. It had taken Vicky some years to realize that though with Mum she felt as she'd imagined she would have with her real mother, with Dad there was almost always a shade of uneasiness. As if she had to be on her best behaviour with him, think before she spoke.

She took the cup to the table and pushed the piled up muddle a little to make room for it. She said awkwardly, "Like me to do anything, Dad?"

He said, "I don't know. Where's Chris?"

"Out with Paul. She won't be back till late. They're going to a concert."

He took the cup of tea and sipped. Vicky stood by the table, uncertain whether her offer had been accepted or not.

"What should happen to Mum's Post Office book? Do you have to give it back?" she asked, seeing a corner of the book half hidden under a sheaf of envelopes, cards and letters.

"Have to close the account. There's her National Insurance card. Have to do something about that too."

He sounded hopeless, as if this sort of practical detail were too much for him. It wasn't like Dad, who was generally good at getting things done, and believed in getting them done promptly. Vicky felt a rush of sympathy for him. He'd known Mum longer than she had. He'd chosen her; for Vicky and Chris she had been a piece of immense luck. At the moment all three of them were feeling as if the centre of their universe had gone. For Chris and herself there would be other, different worlds, new people, new interests, but for Dad that wasn't likely. He would have to get used to living without half of himself.

She sat opposite to him. "Can't I help?"

He said, unwillingly, "Suppose you could look through some of these boxes." He pushed a mound of little cardboard boxes over towards Vicky. She began opening them, one by one. Some were empty of anything more interesting than shreds of yellowing cotton wool. One held the famous garnet brooch, another a string of green glass beads, a third

10

had a Christmas cracker charm, a silver wishbone. Vicky remembered the party at which her Mum had found it in a big red cracker with gold-fringed ends. Beautiful.

She found a couple more empty boxes. Then one containing a carefully tied up wisp of dark hair, not more than half an inch long. Inside the box's lid was written, in Mrs. Stanford's round handwriting, "Vicky's hair, aged one week." Vicky could just imagine her Mum snipping off that tiny portion of baby fluff. She'd always said that Vicky, unlike Chris, had never been bald. She'd looked human from the first. Well, almost human, she'd had to add, laughing. Vicky's eyes pricked.

She looked across at her Dad. He was going through the papers. He'd got some sort of method of sorting them out; there was a pile on his left in which Vicky recognized Mum's Post Office book and her National Insurance card. A lot more he was putting on the other side, letters he just glanced at, yellow folders of snapshots, picture postcards. He was turning a fat envelope upside down on to the table, and she saw him take one look at the contents as they spilled out, and then glance quickly towards her. Their eyes met. She knew that he was wondering if he could shove everything back into the envelope and pretend it had nothing to do with her. But it was too late. He left the papers lying where they had fallen. A couple of smaller envelopes. Something wrapped in tissue paper.

Vicky said, "Dad?"

"What's that?"

"What's in that envelope?" She knew already that it was something that concerned her.

He said slowly, "It's the papers and other things. Mum was keeping them until you were a bit older."

"What papers, Dad?"

"Adoption papers. All that."

"Adoption papers? Anything else?" Vicky asked.

"Not sure." He unfolded the tissue paper. It contained a long tress of straight black hair.

"That's mine!" Vicky exclaimed. Then she said, "Can't be. Mine's never been as long as that."

11

"I remember now. Mum took a lock of your mother's hair. After she'd ... died. Thought maybe you ought to have something so you'd know a bit what she was like."

Mum. Even then she'd known the right thing to do. Vicky said, "Anything else?"

Mr. Stanford pushed the papers across the table. "You'd better look. I know Mum always said there wasn't much to be going on."

He went back to his sorting. Vicky sat for a moment with the contents of the big envelope strewn in front of her. They couldn't tell her much, she thought, that she didn't know already. She'd asked Mum often enough and Mrs. Stanford had told her all she, herself, knew. That there had been no visitors for the girl with the long black hair, whose name probably hadn't been Jenny Morgan, though that was what she'd called herself. That when Mrs. Stanford had asked her, at visiting time, when husbands of all shapes and ages had come to be introduced to the new member of the family, if Mr. Morgan wasn't coming, the girl had said, No, he wasn't. In those days girls with babies didn't often own up to not being married, straight out. Mrs. Stanford had reckoned that very likely Vicky's father didn't even know that Jenny was going to have his baby. Another time she'd asked, "What about your Mum and Dad, what'll they think?" And Jenny Morgan had said, "I haven't got a Mum and Dad. I haven't got anybody. Not really."

"She said you were all the family she'd got. Of course if I'd known what was going to happen, I'd have asked a bit more. But I never dreamed... Then she started feeling bad, and I didn't like to ask a lot of questions." That was what Mum had said. If she'd known any more, she'd have told Vicky. She'd never refused to answer a question. She'd told Vicky about the adoption, how she and Dad had had to answer a lot of questions and fill in a whole lot of forms before they were let to have Vicky for their own.

There had been very few personal belongings. "Just what she'd been wearing when she came into the hospital, and a few little things to put you in when she took you out.

12

To tell you the truth, most of it looked as if it'd come straight from Marks and Sparks, or somewhere like that. Nothing special. Except for the shawl. She'd knitted that herself. I remember her showing it me, and telling me it was the first fancy thing she'd ever knitted. I don't know why, but it makes me cry every time I take it out to see it isn't getting the moth. Suppose it's thinking of how she must have been planning for you, and meaning to be as good a mother as she could be, poor love. I know when I put you in that shawl to bring you back home, I fairly howled. Silly.''

Vicky had seen the shawl. Delicate, a lacy pattern, cobwebs alternating with sea shells. It must have taken ages. She'd seen the clothes too. They looked funny to her now, but that was what everyone was wearing in the sixties, Mum had said. Nothing to give away Jenny Morgan's real identity. No National Insurance card, no diary. She'd walked into the casualty department of St. Clare's hospital one night and had her baby the next day. You couldn't get much more anonymous than Vicky's real mother had managed to be.

"When you're eighteen, love, if you're really set on it, we'll think about doing something to find out," Mum had said, and Vicky had known that she was grateful for the excuse to delay. "Till then you're ours, Dad's and mine," Mum had ended. Vicky had liked that. She could hardly have been more Mum's, if it was warm, unlimited love that counted. But still there was a part of her that remained unsatisfied. She couldn't ever quite forget that she had come, as she thought of it, out of nowhere. She had no family history as other people had. She was haunted by questions. "Where did I really come from? What were they like . . . my mother, my father, their mothers and fathers? Who am I, *really*?'' Sometimes, when the feeling was strongest, she wondered if knowing nothing about her past would mean that her future would be equally dark.

She'd known about the adoption papers, but she'd never actually seen them. She sorted the contents of the big envelope now with anxious fingers, as if she was afraid she might find something that would threaten her.

The adoption papers told her nothing she hadn't always known. There were letters from a firm of solicitors, a summons to court proceedings where the question of her adoption was to be heard and decided. A letter from an adoption society saying that someone was pleased to inform Mrs. Stanford that she and her husband had been approved as suitable parents for adoption and that they would be informed when a baby was available. Vicky didn't understand. She'd been available, hadn't she? Then she saw the date of the letter. More than a year before she and Chris had been born. She remembered now. Mum had told her that she'd had a lot of trouble having a baby. A lot of miscarriages, then nothing. She'd been advised to adopt. Then she'd found she was pregnant again, and this time carried through and had Chris. No wonder she'd been so pleased with her own baby, no wonder she'd insisted on having Vicky too.

There were endless letters from the adoption society and from social workers, some originals, some copies. A receipted bill from the solicitor. Two birth certificates. Two? Did you have to have two if you were adopted? But the first one she looked at turned out to be Chris's. Of course! Mum had kept them all together, making no difference here, as everywhere else, between the two girls. Vicky compared the two certificates. Chris's was all filled out, Mum's and Dad's names and address, Dad's occupation, Mum's name before she married. Chris's full name, Christina Irene. By comparison, Vicky's certificate was sketchy. She had only one name. Victoria. There was no maiden name for her mother. No name for her father. The address given was that of the hospital where she'd been born, St. Clare's. And that was all.

Vicky studied the two forms and wondered why her mother had been so anxious not to be traced. That deliberate concealment of everything she'd been and gone through up to the moment of her baby's birth – what did it mean? Vicky had heard, read often in stories, of girls who first discovered that they were illegitimate when they saw

14

their birth certificates. Then they were always upset, felt disowned and unwanted, wondered if their mothers had been "bad", and thought this made them inferior, degraded. Vicky didn't feel any of that. Probably because of the picture Mrs. Stanford had given her of her real mother: young, intelligent, loving. Mum had said that she reckoned whoever Vicky's father had been, he and her mother must have loved each other. "She was that kind of girl. She wouldn't have gone with a boy she didn't respect." Kind Mum! She'd made sure that from the start Vicky should feel that she'd been wanted. Twice wanted, twice welcomed. First by the girl who hadn't any family except for her baby, and then by Mum herself, who'd learned with sorrow in the hospital that she'd never have another baby after Chris, but who had triumphantly brought home two girls, as she said, 'for the price of one.'

Vicky didn't mind the illegitimacy. Lots of girls nowadays chose to have babies without being married, anyway. She couldn't see that it made any difference to you as a person. It was the gaps in her knowledge of her origins that nagged. Coupled with the feeling of no longer belonging to the family she'd grown up in, as she had while Mum was alive.

There was something else in the envelope. Vicky shook it upside down. An oblong of stiff paper came out and lay on the kitchen table. Vicky turned it over and saw the snapshot of a young man. He stood against a tracery of iron railings, his arm lying along the top bar. He was badly out of focus, or he had moved as the snap was taken. Vicky could only just make out a face constructed on vertical lines, narrow, with a medium nose and dark eyebrows, pulled together as he scowled into the sun. A high forehead was topped by straight darkish hair. He was wearing an open-necked shirt and dark trousers. He could have been any age between eighteen and thirty. Behind him, in startling clarity compared to the blurred figure, quite a way in the distance, was what looked like the side of a tall cliff, part bare, part covered with dark trees. Across the bare face, running diagonally downwards from left to right, were the

15

lines of the strata, showing that at some period, a millennium ago, this particular landscape had been violently thrown around. On the top of the cliff, almost out of the picture, was a tiny round building, a tower, with a little knob atop, like a child's toy.

Vicky turned it over again. Nothing written on the back, no name, no date. Nothing to show where the snapshot had been taken, or for whom it had been meant. She gazed at the indistinct figure and thought, "Is that my father?"

She said, "Dad!" and Mr. Stanford looked up.

"Who's this?" She passed it across the table.

"I don't know. Where'd you find it?"

"In the big envelope. With our birth certificates."

He studied the picture more closely. "Never seen the fellow, so far's I know. Not that it's easy to see, that small and smudgy."

"Could it be Uncle Jimmy?" One of Mum's brothers had been killed in the war.

"Jimmy had curly hair. He wasn't as tall as this boy, anyway."

"Didn't Mum ever tell you anything about it? The picture?" Vicky asked.

"Not that I remember." He pushed it back towards her.

"Dad!"

"What?"

She didn't know how to express what she wanted to say. "If it was in the envelope, with our certificates, and things. Do you think...?"

"Do I think what? Say what you mean straight out."

"D'you think it's something to do with my mother? I mean ... like a relation?"

"How'd I know? Told you, I never saw it before."

"Can I have it?" Vicky asked.

He hesitated. Then, "Yes, I suppose so. You better ask Chris if she knows anything about it. Don't throw it out, that's all."

"What shall I do with all this? Our certificates and all that?"

16

"I'll keep them. That way I'll know where they are when they're wanted."

Vicky put the papers back in the envelope and laid it flat on the table.

"You want this?" Mr. Stanford asked her, picking up the tissue paper parcel of the black hair.

"Please."

His expression as he handed it to her was neutral, gave nothing away. She put the faded snapshot on top of the white paper and stood up.

"Where'll you keep it?" Mr. Stanford asked.

"In my room. I've got a box."

She and Chris each had a box for things they wanted to keep entirely to themselves. They were scrupulous about never looking in each others', though they were ordinary cardboard boxes, no keys, not even tied round with string. Vicky didn't know what Chris kept in hers. She herself had nearly all the poems she'd ever written, bits she'd cut out of magazines and papers, shells she'd collected from a seaside holiday, the programme of a pop concert she'd been taken to by a boy she'd fancied for a time, relics of childhood like a tiny plush kitten, loved bald, a baby silver bracelet she could no longer slip over her hand. Nothing of any real value except to her; her treasures, they represented a fair proportion of her life up till now.

Alone upstairs in the room she and Chris shared, Vicky looked again at the picture of the young man, and then at her own face in the glass. Was there any resemblance at all? Vicky couldn't be sure. She wasn't sure, either, whether she wanted to find a resemblance or not. She put the photograph and the lock of hair in her box, feeling disturbed. Bits of the past which might or mightn't fit together, which raised all the questions which Mum had wanted to put off for the present, and which she'd thought might never be answered. "We tried, really we did, Vicky. Had to, before we were allowed to get you for keeps. And that's years ago. It isn't going to be any easier now," she'd said.

Vicky had a flush of anger against the girl who had blotted out everything connected with her past, denying

17

her daughter the right to claim anything for her own. It wasn't fair to put a baby into the world and then to leave it with nothing but a single name, an anonymous photograph and a length of dark hair. The Mum she had known would never have done a cruel thing like that.

3

The next day, Monday, after they'd got back from school, Vicky fetched the snapshot from her box and brought it down to the kitchen, where they were doing their homework. She put it down in front of Chris.

"Know who that is?"

Chris studied the square of paper.

"Not the faintest. Who is it?"

"That's what I want to know."

"Suppose it could be someone like Henry Fonda ages ago. When he was young. Where'd you get it, anyway?"

"It was in with the papers Mum kept in that drawer. Birth certificates and that."

Chris saw the significance of this. She said, "You mean it might be a relation? Or something?"

"That's why I wondered if you knew."

Chris looked at the faded young man by the railings again.

"I'm sure I've never seen this photo before."

"Dad says it isn't Uncle Jimmy."

"Well, it certainly isn't Uncle Ted."

Vicky laughed. Uncle Ted was enormous, a barrel of a man. Photos of him at the age of twelve showed that he'd been outsize even then.

"Who, then? Didn't Dad have any idea?" Chris asked.

"Said he'd never seen it before."

"It isn't like anyone in Mum's family. They all had roundish sort of faces. And curly hair," Chris said.

19

With difficulty, Vicky said, "Is it like me?"

Chris held the snapshot at arm's length. Her eyes went from the tiny, blurred face above the railings to Vicky's, close, distinct, troubled. She said, "Honestly, I can't tell. It's difficult to see."

"Could it be like me?" Vicky insisted.

"It could. Only not so that anyone would stop and say, 'That must be someone in the family.' Do you want it to be?"

"I don't know. Yes. In a sort of way. I can't help thinking, 'Suppose, that's my father.'"

Chris turned the photo over, as Vicky had done. "No name. Not even a date. Could be your grandfather."

She hadn't thought of that. "Wouldn't he look different? Have different sort of hair? Or a beard or something?"

"Not a beard. Think of Grandpa Lawes. Those old photos of him. He looked just like this. I mean, hair and clothes and things."

It was true. Vicky said, "Do people have photos of their fathers? To carry around?"

"Why not? Or a brother. Or a boy-friend, another one. Not . . ." She didn't finish the sentence.

Vicky took the snapshot back into her own hands. "I wish I knew."

"You can't tell anything from that. Not what he really looked like," Chris said.

"No. But. Someone might recognize it."

"You said Dad didn't."

"I mean someone we don't know about. Anyone."

"Who?"

"I don't know. I mean, anyone who saw it in a paper. Or on television or something."

Chris was silent.

"You know. Like they show photos of people who are missing. Girls, sometimes. They say, 'If anyone recognizes this person, please get in touch with the police,' or something like that."

Chris still didn't speak.

"What's the matter?" Vicky asked, impatient.

"It's just. It sounds . . . as if you didn't want to belong here any more."

"It isn't that! You know it isn't. It isn't like that!"

"Then . . .? Can't you leave it alone? It isn't like looking for your real mother, or not knowing why she'd let you be adopted, if she was still alive. You know about her."

"I don't! I just know she's dead, that's all. I don't know where she came from or what she was like, or anything."

"Why does it matter so much? It doesn't to us. Dad and me."

Vicky had tried to explain this before. She tried again. "It isn't that I don't want to belong here. It's just that I feel . . ."

"What?"

"As if I'd lost something. Only I've never had it. It's like not having any roots. No. That's not it. It isn't roots, exactly. It's not knowing what sort of people they were. My family. It's like being a plant that's got planted somewhere, but no one knows what sort of plant it's going to turn out to be. As if you'd lost the seed packet." She said again, desperately. "It's the not *knowing*, Chris. You must see."

"Mum didn't want you to try to find out," Chris said, as if she hadn't heard this.

"She didn't mind. She always said, when I was eighteen . . ."

"I think that's why she didn't show you that photograph."

"That's silly. You said, it wouldn't help."

"You know she didn't like it when you used to talk about going to look for your father."

"I said, she didn't really mind," Vicky said.

"Yes, she did. She may not have told you, but I know she did. It made her feel . . ."

"What?"

"As if we weren't good enough for you."

"That's stupid! I never said . . ."

"You think it, though. I know you do. You probably think you'll find out that your family's rich or famous. Or something."

"I don't!" Vicky cried.

21

"Then why do you go on about it? As if having Mum wasn't enough?"

"I never said that!"

"It makes me feel as if you couldn't wait to get away from here. I'd have thought you might want to do what Mum'd have wanted. It's like as if now she's dead, you want to rush off and find another family."

"Chris!"

"I'm going upstairs," Chris said abruptly.

"You can't! It's freezing . . ." But Chris had gone, shutting the door behind her with a bang.

Vicky got up to follow her. Then sat down again, miserable. She and Chris didn't often quarrel. Of course they got irritated with each other, and snapped, but since they'd been small they hadn't had a real row like this. When they'd been kids, they'd fought about silly little things, first turn on the swing, who should lick out Mum's mixing bowl. But today she'd really hurt Chris's feelings, and Vicky knew that it wasn't so much that she felt herself rejected by Vicky's attitude. It was Mum. Vicky understood this. She'd have felt the same. She'd have fought just as fiercely if anyone had seemed to imply that Mum had been anything but the best mother anyone could ever possibly have. Just as Chris was the best sister. But knowing this didn't quieten the questioning voice inside Vicky's mind. That was what she couldn't, it seemed, explain without hurting the people who made up her world.

The terrible thing was that in a way Chris had been right. Not that Vicky couldn't wait to get away from being a Stanford, but that she had fantasies about her real family. Of course she had sometimes wondered if they were rich, or famous, or if she mightn't turn out to be the heiress to a fortune or a wonderful house or a great estate. If you'd read almost any sort of story in books and magazines, you couldn't help that sort of idea coming into your mind. But it was nonsense, and Vicky knew that it was nonsense. And it wasn't that sort of fantasy that haunted her. She didn't want to give up being what she was, Chris's sister, Mum's and Dad's daughter; she wanted to add to what she'd already got, to fill in the background, to make a whole of her fragmented history.

She couldn't go back to homework with the quarrel un-made-up. She went up into their room and found Chris tidying her side of the wardrobe they shared. Vicky put her arms round her and said, "Chris. I'm sorry."

Chris had been crying. Her eyes were still red. She turned in Vicky's arms and rubbed her cheek against Vicky's. "I'm sorry too. I shouldn't have said all that. It wasn't fair."

"You do know, I thought Mum was. . . ."

"Of course I know. And I do understand. A bit, anyway."

"It's not that she and you and Dad aren't good enough. It's just about the not knowing . . ."

"I do know. Really."

"Sometimes I think p'raps my real father was a drop-out. Or a hippy. There were lots of hippies then."

"I don't care what he was," Chris said.

"He might be in prison."

"I didn't mean Mum didn't understand how you felt. She knew you'd never stop loving all of us."

They both cried a little.

"We'd better go down and get on with our homework before Dad gets back," Chris said.

"He'll see I've been crying. I look terrible for hours."

"No, he won't."

"Sure?"

"He doesn't look at us much." Chris said it as a simple statement of fact, without rancour.

"It's worse for him than for us, even," Vicky said.

"Of course it is. That's why . . ."

"Why what?"

"Don't say any more about that photograph to him. Or how you feel. You know."

4

Chris and Vicky came home on the last day of the school term, weighed down with books and notes. The Easter holidays were only three weeks long, but they'd been given enough work to last a year, whereas the "O" Level exams began in less than three months.

Vicky made herself a list of all she was supposed to get through. She groaned.

"I'll never do it, if I work eight hours a day. Might as well not be on holiday."

"I don't believe we will do eight hours a day. Not at home. We don't do that even in term time," Chris said.

"That makes it worse. Then I'll feel guilty all the time," Vicky said.

"You shouldn't worry. Everyone says you're sure to pass. Five of them anyway, and that's all that matters."

"I don't want to fail any," Vicky said.

"I didn't mean you'd fail. I just meant you'll get enough passes to do whatever you want afterwards."

Passes were not all that Vicky wanted, but she didn't say so. Instead she said, "I'm going to make a huge great calendar of all the days till the end of the exams and cross one off every day. That'll make it not seem so long."

"I'd have thought it'd seem longer," Chris said.

"Well, anyway." But while she was drawing ruled lines on the largest sheet of paper she could find, and dividing the compartments into weeks and months, Vicky knew quite well that what she was doing was an elaborate piece of self-deception, spending an hour on a neat, impressive-looking and utterly useless catalogue of time.

She pushed it away, half finished. Chris looked up from the opposite side of the kitchen table.

"You're right. It makes it look worse," Vicky said.

"Eleven weeks. Nearly," Chris said.

"I suppose the moment we've finished this lot, they'll start telling us what we've got to do for 'A's," Vicky said, grumbling.

There was a short silence. As Vicky pulled the geometry book towards her, Chris said, "I'm not sure I'm going to stay on and take 'A's."

Vicky stared.

"You must!"

"I don't have to."

"But . . . we always said we would."

"I knew you would. I've never made up my mind about me."

"I can't stay on without you!" Vicky said.

"Don't be silly. Of course you could."

Chris didn't sound upset. She looked as calm as ever.

"What would you do if you left? You mean at the end of the term?"

"I haven't decided."

"You mean . . . go to the Tech. and do a course there?'

"I might," Chris said.

"What sort of course?" Vicky asked, trying to appear sympathetic, when what she was feeling was hurt, angry, miserable. Chris must have thought all this out, had been considering, making up her mind to this revolutionary action for ages, and had never said a word about it.

"I might take the secretarial course. Mrs. Stelling says that's a good start for almost everything. Only I don't think I will," Chris said.

"What will you do, then?"

"I wouldn't mind doing nursery nursing. I like babies," Chris said.

"You could do your 'A's first and that after."

"It'd be a waste of time," Chris said, and Vicky thought,

25

"It's because of Paul. She means to marry him and have lots of babies. Having 'A' levels wouldn't matter then." She wanted to say something hurtful, like "Suppose you don't have any babies yourself?" or "Suppose you need to get a job after you're married?" But she didn't. She didn't want another quarrel. Chris said, "Vicky?"

"What?"

"Don't mind so much. We'll still be here together, even if I do go to the Tech. It isn't as if we saw all that much of each other in school anyway."

Vicky said, "It makes me feel as if we're different."

"We are. You've always been cleverer than me."

"Only at some things."

"But you . . ." Chris struggled for the right words. "You really like school work. I like ordinary things. I mean, *things*. Not ideas about things so much."

"You like history. You've always been good at that."

"That's real things, isn't it? And it doesn't have poetry, or trying to see what someone means when they write something. I mean, it really happened. That's what I like."

"Is geometry real?" Vicky asked, looking at the page in front of her, all lines and angles and "therefores" and "equals" and "Q.E.D.s".

Surprisingly, Chris said, "Sort of. If you're doing that too, let's learn theorems and test each other. It's better than trying to do them alone."

It was the way they'd generally done their homework. But below the surface of her mind, taken up with isosceles triangles and parallelograms, Vicky could feel the hurt and the knowledge that Chris had not denied the difference between them as she would have a year ago. She had, instead, almost deliberately, widened the gap.

This had been a Wednesday. Two days later, Vicky was alone in the kitchen, pretending to work, but with the radio on (the television programme couldn't have been excused as background music) when the bell rang. Opening the door, she saw Stephen.

"Hi!" he said.

Vicky said, "Come in!"

"Sure I'm not interrupting?" Stephen asked.

"There's only me at home. Come on." She led the way back into the kitchen. Stephen followed.

"You're working," he said, seeing the books open on the table.

"Sort of." She switched off the radio. "But it's nice to be interrupted sometimes. I can't work straight through all the time. Not properly."

"I don't believe anyone does. People say they've been reading for ten hours, but I bet it isn't real work. You know – I've often sat in front of a book for ages and then suddenly I know I haven't taken in a word, I've been thinking about something quite different."

"I seem to do that a lot," Vicky said. It was true of what they were doing now, too, she thought. They might seem to be talking about work or not work, but what they were really thinking about was Vicky's Mum. Because they hadn't met to speak to each other since Mum had died. There ought to be words which they could exchange on this occasion, but she couldn't think of any.

"Have a cup of tea? Or would you rather have coffee?" was the best she could do.

"Coffee'd be great," Stephen said, sitting at the table. He could feel Vicky's unease and guessed that she was afraid he'd begin talking about Mrs. Stanford's death. Or, on the other hand, she might want him to say something. Hell! Stephen thought, as he'd often done before, how much easier it would be to be the sort of person who didn't think too carefully before he spoke. Now, whatever he did, he'd do it awkwardly.

She was standing by the cooker with her back to him. Easier to speak when she wasn't too near and looking at him. He said, "I should've written to you about your mother. I'm sorry I didn't."

"I saw you at the funeral," she said.

"I meant to come back here afterwards. But then ... I didn't. There were such a lot of people."

"It wouldn't have been any good you coming back," she said.

"Is it . . .?" He didn't know how to say what he wanted to, but Vicky understood.

"It's horrible. I didn't know before how Mum . . ."

"She was," Stephen said.

After a moment, he asked, "How's Chris?"

"Chris is all right. As much as she can be."

"Something's wrong?"

Vicky poured the boiling water into two mugs and stirred until the liquid was dark and clear. She added milk and said, "One lump or two?" before she answered his question. "Why should anything be wrong?"

"You said that about Chris being all right as if . . . I don't know. As if she shouldn't be."

Vicky took a sip of coffee. A loud sip, because it was hot. She said, "I didn't mean she shouldn't be all right. She's missing Mum. Of course. It's just that . . . everything's different."

"You and Chris?"

"She doesn't talk to me like she used to."

"How d'you mean?"

"She'll come out with something she's been thinking for ages and hasn't said."

"Everyone does that, don't they?" Stephen said, remembering the countless thoughts he had about his parents, his friends, life in general, which he kept mostly to himself.

Vicky said, resentfully, "Not like that. Chris didn't, anyway. I always knew what she was thinking about. She used to say."

"Did you?" Stephen said.

"I did. I don't now. But that's because there are things Chris doesn't want me to talk about."

"What sort of things?"

Vicky looked across the table at him. Had he ever noticed before how dark the lashes were round her greenery-yallery eyes? Cat's eyes, surprising with all that nearly black hair. She seemed to be considering whether to answer his question. At last she said, "If I say anything

28

about wanting to find out about my . . . my real family. I mean my real mother.If I say anything, Chris gets upset. She thinks I'm saying she and Dad aren't good enough."

"I see. Especially now," Stephen said.

"She never used to be like that."

"She didn't feel she had to fight for your mother . . . I mean, her mother . . . before," Stephen said.

"That's it! And Dad would be the same. No, he'd be worse. I don't see how I'd ever talk about it to him."

"Must be difficult."

"It's the not being able to talk about it to anyone. It makes me feel as if I shouldn't be thinking it."

"You can talk to me. It won't hurt my feelings," Stephen said.

Vicky said, "Thanks," and there was a silence.

"Go on," Stephen said.

"I don't know where to begin."

"I know you've always wondered about your real mother and father. You told me." It had been her first confidence to him, and had made him warm towards her. It had been at that moment that he had begun to lose the resentment he'd felt on their first acquaintanceship when they'd discovered the uncomfortable, inexplicable link between them. They had been strangers, had never so much as spoken to each other when they'd discovered that they shared sudden, frightening flashes of vision which showed them events which had not yet happened. A street accident, a baby stolen from its pram. A van driving too fast by the edge of a wild grey sea towards dangerous cliffs and the darkness in which a murder had been planned.

"Since Mum died, I've been thinking. When she was there, I could ask her any time. About my real mother, I mean. Now I can't. There might be things she could've told me, no one else could. She was the only one who ever saw my mother to talk to."

"I expect you did really ask all the questions you could. It's because you know you can't ask any more that you feel like that."

Vicky said, "I suppose so. Only . . . Now there's a

29

photograph I didn't know about before. It was with the things that Mum had kept. That belonged to my mother."

"A photograph of who? Could it be your mother?" Stephen asked.

"It's a man. Wait a moment. I'll show you."

Stephen heard her run up the stairs, taking two steps at a time. When she returned she was carrying an envelope. She tipped the contents out on to the table in front of him.

He picked up the photograph and studied it.

"It's not a bit like you."

"But someone might recognize it."

"Who? Who could you show it to?"

"You see photos in the papers sometimes. Or on the telly. When a person's missing."

"But..." Stephen hated the idea. "It's terribly public. Your Dad wouldn't like it. Nor would Chris, would she?"

Vicky shook her head.

"What about the hospital? Where you were born. Wouldn't someone there know something?" Stephen asked.

"Mum said everyone got asked a lot of questions before she was allowed to take me."

"No, I meant, mightn't one of the doctors remember something? Or a nurse or somebody? After all, not many people die having babies nowadays," Stephen said.

"But if all they remembered was her dying..." Vicky said.

"Just because she died, someone might remember something about her. You know how people do. If someone has an accident or wins the pools or something, even if you don't ever see them again, you sort of think..."

"I know. People say, 'And to think, only the day before she was telling me...'" Vicky said.

"Yes. Like that."

"How'd I ever find a nurse who was there sixteen years ago?" Vicky asked.

"There must be some other way," Stephen said.

They looked at each other, remembering.

"We could..." Stephen began.

"It wouldn't work," Vicky said, quickly.

"It did before."

"Yes . . . But. It worked forwards, didn't it? I mean, we saw what was going to happen. What I want to know now is what happened ages ago."

"You've still got your bit of the Egg, have you?" Stephen asked.

"Mm." Vicky saw it in her mind's eye, her fragment of the Chinese puzzle Egg. It was upstairs, in her box. She knew exactly where it lay, wrapped in silver foil. "As if you were going to cook it!" Chris had said, when she'd seen Vicky lapping it in silver. Even to Chris, Vicky couldn't explain. Silver was a charm against witchcraft. It took a silver bullet to kill a witch. Vicky had had the ridiculous idea that silver foil might somehow insulate the power of her piece of the Egg. Like covering uranium in lead.

"If you did ever want to try . . . I've got all my bits at home," Stephen said.

Vicky looked at him doubtfully. "It made me feel . . . peculiar."

"Abnormal," said Stephen, the psychiatrist's son.

"I didn't like it."

"I didn't, either. Only I don't think it's all that peculiar. Dad was telling me the other day about people who do experiments on things like that. They call it parapsychology."

"You mean other people can see what's going to happen like we did?" Vicky asked.

"Sort of. Only they do it in labs and it's all controlled. They have two people in different rooms, and one of them turns up playing cards and the other one has to say what the card is going to be."

"I don't see what use that is," Vicky said.

"It's to make it a proper scientific experiment," Stephen said. He wasn't sure whether he was trying to reassure Vicky or himself. He wished he could think of some positive way of helping her, which didn't involve using again what had seemed like the magic properties of the Chinese Egg.

With a sudden inspiration, he said, "I know! Price!"

"Price? What of?"

"Not of anything. Detective Chief Superintendent Price. The one who found the Wilmington baby."

"Oh! Him. What about him?"

"Why don't you ask him? How to start trying to find out about your mother. How people find out that sort of thing. He must know."

"You don't think he'd mind?" But she looked encouraged.

"I'm sure he wouldn't. He liked you."

"How'd I ask him?"

"You could go and see him at New Scotland Yard," Stephen said.

"Without saying I was going or anything?"

"He can always say he can't see you. Or that he wouldn't be able to do anything."

She considered this. "I suppose I might. It'd be something to try. Better than just sitting about and thinking. He'd know about getting a photo published, too. Wouldn't he?"

"You wouldn't, really. Would you?"

"No. You're right. I couldn't do that to Chris and Dad."

She looked down at the photograph, lying between them. Stephen, following the direction of her eyes, said, "What's that behind him?"

"The railings, d'you mean?" She'd concentrated on the figure and hadn't given much thought to the background.

"That's an enormous cliff, isn't it?" Stephen said.

"Those railings. Could it be a pier? Only there doesn't seem to be any sea."

"More likely a bridge. There're those upright things, see? Going up from the railings. You don't get them on piers."

"Mightn't you, if there's a roof? Some piers do have roofs, don't they?"

"But the sun's out. I mean, he's right in the sun, isn't he? He wouldn't be if he was under a roof. And anyway, there'd be sea, like you said."

Vicky saw that he was right. "A bridge across what? Why can't you see a river or something?"

"It must be terrifically deep. Like a canyon. Perhaps it's in America," Stephen said. He saw Vicky's face fall and said, "It doesn't have to be. There must be places in England where there are bridges across valleys. Someone must know. There can't be that many."

"But . . ."

"Shall I try to find out? It just might be a help, mightn't it?" Stephen said.

"How would you find out?"

"Someone might recognize it. Or there must be books about bridges. For engineers. Anyway, that cliff, with those sort of lines going across it, and that comic little thing on top. There can't be many places that have got all those things together."

"No – o." But she sounded doubtful.

"Would you like me to try to find out?" he asked.

"Would you really? Wouldn't it be a nuisance?"

"I may not find anything," Stephen said, foreseeing failure and disappointment, now he'd made the offer.

"It'd be great if you would, though."

"Can I borrow it? I'll be very careful. Promise."

She hesitated. He said, "Look, I'll get a Xerox copy and send it back. Won't that do?"

She handed him the snapshot and he put it carefully in his wallet. Looking at what remained on the table, he asked, "What's the other thing you brought down? That, in paper?"

Vicky unfolded the tissue paper and drew out the long tress of dark hair.

"Dad says Mum cut it off after my mother died, so she could show me. Only she never did. I found it in the envelope with the photo. It's beautiful, isn't it?"

Stephen touched it lightly with a finger-tip. "It's exactly like yours."

5

Detective Chief Superintendent James Price sat in his office in New Scotland Yard, trying to make sense out of more than twenty depositions taken from people who might or might not have been involved in a peculiarly ingenious and violent bank robbery. He had to make up his mind which of the speakers had been telling the truth, or how much of it. Then there were the witnesses. It wasn't easy. He wished that people making statements would stick to the point, refuse to allow their minds to wander off to side issues. His task would have been so much easier if the witnesses in this particular case hadn't insisted on a hundred irrelevant details. There were situations, of course, in which the day of the week, or the weather, did matter. And if it had here, he was willing to bet that no one would have come forward with a clear memory of either.

He looked out of his fifteenth floor window. Over London he could see an April sky: pale blue, with small white clouds racing across it. The next weekend it would be Easter and he'd have a day or two off, if he was lucky. He must try to do something about the garden. Plant out the bean seedlings which were cluttering up his tiny kitchen. Get in a good long walk by the canal. Forget, if he could, about stupid criminals and scatty witnesses, and be himself, Jim Price, middle-aged, lonely, fed up a lot of the time with the job, assailed by longings which he seldom let himself formulate. Restless, but not dissatisfied enough to take a gamble and opt for something quite different. Not yet.

34

It was the spring. Or the seven year itch. He ran his fingers through his hair and turned back to the mountain of paper on his desk.

The telephone at his elbow shrilled. Internal phone. He picked up the receiver, noting with a sort of amusement that although he had insisted he was not to be disturbed, he was in fact grateful for the interruption. It was the desk downstairs by the main entrance.

"There's a girl here says she wants to see you, sir."

Price heard himself bark. "What girl?"

"Says you know her, sir."

"What's her name, idiot?"

There was a murmured colloquy the other end of the line. "Stanford. Miss Stanford."

"I don't know anyone of that name," Price said, and was just about to bang the receiver back, when a thought struck him. "Did you say Stanford? Ask her what her first name is."

Another murmur in the background. "Says it's Vicky, sir."

"Right. Ask her to wait. I'll send someone down to bring her up," Price said. He got up and opened the door into the general office next door. "There's a Miss Stanford down in the Back Hall. Bring her up, somebody, will you?" he said, and went back to his desk, wondering how it was that the name of the Back Hall had survived the move from the old building and still, inconsequently, was what the front, main entrance was always called.

He wondered, too, during the minutes it took for his Sergeant to go down and to bring Vicky up in the not always reliable lifts, what she wanted. He hoped she wasn't coming with a story as difficult to believe as the one she and the boy, Stephen, had come up with that first time they'd made contact with him at the beginning of the Wilmington case. Impossible, he'd have thought. But there must have been something there; whether you called it extra-sensory perception, or telepathy, or whatever, didn't make any difference to the fact that it had worked. Without those two, he doubted if he'd have been able to rescue that

35

small girl. Some things you just had to accept, however annoying it was not to be able to explain them in the light of reason.

There was a tap on his door, and Sergeant Peabody, rather pink in the face, showed Vicky in. His first impression was that she was exactly the same. His second was of a profound change.

The child Vicky whom he'd last seen had had bony features a little too large for her face. She moved awkwardly sometimes, not yet knowing how to relate to the space her body occupied, or what to do with her hands. This girl walked into his room like a young princess. It was only in her glance at him, questioning, uncertain, that he recognized the younger Vicky, and saw that her confidence was still half assumed, not yet built-in. He saw something else at the same time, which astonished him. He'd thought, when he'd known her before, that, in spite of having an interesting face, intelligent and sensitive, she wasn't a patch on her sister, Chris, for looks. Chris, he remembered, had been outstandingly pretty. But Vicky, it was now clear to him, might at any moment – and perhaps only for moments at a time – flare into beauty.

He'd stood up as she came into the room. Now he held out his hand.

"Vicky! It's good to see you. Sit down." To Sergeant Peabody at the door, he said, "Jill! Could you bring us two cups of coffee?"

When she'd shut the door behind her, he looked again at Vicky. He saw that she wasn't ready yet to tell him why she was there. He pushed the papers on the desk away from him and said, "It must be two years since I saw you. Tell me about yourself. What's been happening to you?"

After a moment's pause, she said, "My Mum died. In February."

He exclaimed. Then said, gently, "That must be very bad. For all of you."

"The only thing was, she wasn't ill. It was sudden. Just after she'd been cooking the supper."

"I'm afraid that must have been a terrible shock?"

36

She said, "Yes. It was."

"How's your father?" Price asked. He didn't remember that he'd ever met Mr. Stanford, but he could believe that anyone married to Vicky's Mum would be broken, for a time at any rate, by her loss.

"He's not too bad. He's busy, that's one thing. But it's terrible for him," Vicky said.

Sergeant Peabody appeared with two cups of coffee. Proper cups, with saucers and metal spoons. She knew what Price thought of cardboard beakers and plastic cutlery.

Sergeant Peabody hovered. She knew that if this was an official visit, it would be her duty to stay, unobtrusively. Chaperone and protector. Price smiled at her.

"You needn't stay, Jill. Miss Stanford is an old friend. I don't think she's come to see me officially. Have you?" he asked Vicky, and was surprised to see her hesitate.

"Is it an official visit?" he asked.

"Not really."

He nodded at Jill Peabody and she shut the door behind her.

"Well, Vicky! Tell me what I can do for you?"

There was a long silence. Then she said, "You know how to find missing people, don't you?"

He thought she was referring to the kidnapping case in which she'd been involved. "Like the Wilmington baby?"

"No. I meant, people who've disappeared. Gone off on their own."

"You mean, run away from home? Or left their husbands or wives? That sort of thing?"

"Yes. Like that."

"We deal with that sort of case, yes. Mind you, there has to be some good reason for us to take a hand. Suspicion of foul play, or if we think someone might be in moral danger. If a young girl goes off to the city without telling her parents where she's going to stay, then we'd make an effort to find her. In case she gets picked up by the wrong sort of person."

37

She thought for a minute. "Suppose it was the other way round? If it was the girl who'd left home, who wanted to find out where her parents were?"

"She'd know, wouldn't she? Where they'd lived when she left?"

"They might have moved away and not left any address."

He considered. "Yes. That does happen. There was a case not long ago. Two old brothers. One had emigrated to the States sixty years back, when he was a lad. Came back to this country and found the family all gone from the place in Kent they'd been living in . . ."

"So how did he find them?" Vicky asked.

"Advertised. In the papers. I think they put out an appeal on the TV networks too. Didn't take long. You might have seen a picture of the two old brothers meeting. It was on all the front pages."

She didn't appear to be listening. He said, gently, "What's all this about, Vicky?"

She said, "Did you know I was adopted?" She didn't wait for an answer but went on quickly, anxious to get it all out, Price saw. "My mother and Mum – Chris's Mum . . . were in the next beds to each other in the hospital. Chris and I were born the same day. Then my mother got ill and died and no one knew where she'd come from or who she was, so Mum took me home and adopted me."

Price saw her look at him defiantly, as if she was daring him to express pity or horror. Or what? He didn't know. He said, "No, I didn't know. She was a wonderful woman, your Mum," and saw with relief that he'd said the right thing.

"Only now . . . I'd like to try to find out about my mother. My real mother."

"You said she died?" Price said, not because he didn't know, but to give himself time.

"Two days after she'd had me. And no one could find out anything about her. Mum thought she didn't give her own name to the hospital or on my birth certificate. They did try to find out where she'd come from and if she had any relations. They had to, because of Mum wanting to adopt me. But there wasn't anyone."

"Do you know what steps they took to trace her . . . your mother?" Price asked.

"No. Mum said they did everything they could think of. But she said, if it wasn't her real name, it'd have been difficult."

"And she didn't leave anything that could have helped?"

"Not really. Just her clothes. Mum said they could have come from anywhere. And . . ." She felt embarrassed by the thought of telling him about the lock of hair. She said, "There was a photograph." She fumbled in a pocket and put the Xerox of the snapshot in front of Price.

He took his time studying it. Too small and faded to be a good likeness or to make it probable that even if it were exposed on the media, anyone would recognise it. Especially at this distance of time. And anyway. The publicity, if this picture were to appear in the popular press, or on the box, would be something he wouldn't want to expose the Stanfords to. He could imagine what a meal some unscrupulous journalist could make out of Vicky's story. Not only that, but the results, if there were any, might be even worse. Who knew what sort of parentage she might discover?

He said, "Your mother doesn't seem to have wanted to be tracked down, does she?"

Vicky said, "She wasn't married. Mum was sure, from what she said. And she said she hadn't any family. Except for me."

"Do you know if she meant to let you go for adoption?" Price asked.

"She meant to keep me. She told Mum that, too."

"That was very brave of her," Price said. Vicky rewarded him with a flashing look of gratitude.

"Mum said it wasn't so easy then, having a baby without being married. She thought that was why my mother probably wasn't using her own name. She said she thought she might not have told him . . . my father . . . anything about me. I mean, that she was going to have a baby. So she wouldn't have wanted anyone to find out about her. In case they told him," Vicky confusedly explained.

Price found it possible now to say, "Vicky, have you thought that if that's right, he might not want to know now? He might even not admit that you were his daughter? Even if you could find him."

"I thought there were tests? Blood tests. Or something," Vicky said.

"There are tests. But they can't prove for certain that a man must be the father of a child. They can prove that he couldn't possibly be, or that he could. But not definitely that he is."

She was silent.

"It's a tricky business, tracing a family. Often it turns out disappointing. Sometimes when a young girl's had a baby and had it adopted, she wants to forget the whole thing. Then, later on, if she's married and has another family of her own, she may not want to be reminded. She doesn't want that first child coming to see her. She may be like your mother, she's gone somewhere she isn't known and she's never told anyone about it. It can make trouble with a husband, who's never suspected she's had a boy-friend before she met him – let alone a baby. You have to remember that, Vicky."

"But my mother's dead! She hasn't got a husband or anyone who'd be upset!" Vicky said.

"If your Mum was right, she hadn't any of the other kind of family either. Parent, or brothers and sisters. So what are you going to look for?" Price asked.

"My father. If I knew who she was, I might find him," Vicky said.

"The same might be true of him. He might have another family now."

"I want to *know*," Vicky said. It was always the same. People seemed to believe that she wanted *things*. Relations, a family, to be acknowledged. And, of course, these were things she would like. But they weren't the most important. She was surprised to see Detective Chief Superintendent Price nod his head. He said, "Yes, I understand that.

40

It's the knowing you need. You feel you have to find out about your family background so that you know what sort of person you are yourself."

"Yes! How did you guess?" Vicky asked.

"We all need to know something about our roots," Price said. Thinking to himself, "if it's only so we know what to get rid of, what to look out for. Danger signals." He thought of his father, coming home drunk more nights than not. Of his washed-out, querulous mother, of the string of younger brothers and sisters for whom he'd felt resentfully responsible. It had probably been that feckless, chaotic household which had made him opt for the Force when he was old enough to leave school. Law and Order, that was what he had wanted then. Which was perhaps why now, after thirty years of trying to impose them on others, he wanted a bit of liberty, a bit of recklessness, before it was too late.

"You aren't adopted too?" Vicky asked.

"No." He'd often had fantasies, though, of really belonging to a quite different sort of family. One he needn't be ashamed of. When he'd been at school he'd told an endless series of imaginative lies to the other children about his parents and his home. He'd taken good care never to let them visit him there. Trouble was, his younger brothers hadn't bothered to keep up the illusion. Jimmy Price had been convicted of being a bloody liar. He remembered the shame to this day.

"Then how do you know?" she was asking, eyes wide with surprise.

He laughed. "A bit of experience, and a bit of imagination. It's not that hard."

"Other people don't understand always," Vicky said.

Price returned to the present. "Look, Vicky. When you're eighteen, you can ask to see your original birth certificate . . ."

"I've seen it. Dad's got it," she interrupted.

"Yes. Well, then. As I was saying, when you're eighteen you can go to the General Register Office and they'll help you. It doesn't sound to me as if there was much infor-

41

mation to go on. It isn't as if your adoption had been the ordinary kind, when the adoption society, or whoever's arranged it, keeps the details of the child's parentage. No one seems to know anything about your background. But still, the General Office might be able to help. That seems to me your most likely chance of finding out. . . ."

She interrupted him again. "Why only when I'm eighteen? Why can't I go to the office, whatever it is, now?"

"Because until you're eighteen they can't help you. They're not allowed to. It's the law."

He saw that this was a new shock for her. He said quickly, "Vicky, don't! It isn't that bad. How old are you now? It only means putting it off for a little."

"Nearly two years!" she shot at him.

"You're sixteen? I'd forgotten." He saw that it would be unkind to pretend that two years didn't look to her, at this moment, as bad as twenty. He waited for her to recover herself.

"There must be something I can do," she said at last.

He tried to think of some grain of comfort he could offer; of any action he could suggest which would satisfy her now without too much risk of disappointment. But no inspiration came to him. He felt, however, that he couldn't send her away like this, having done nothing but discourage her. He said, "I'll think about it. If anything comes up that I think might help, I'll let you know."

He managed to convey by the tone of his voice that the interview was at an end. She was as responsive as ever. She stood up, and with another of those touching approaches towards maturity, she held out her hand and said, "You've been very kind. Thank you."

He shook the hand. It was cold. He said, "I'll see you down."

Sergeant Peabody, carrying more cups of coffee, was surprised to see him conduct the schoolgirl to the lift and then go down with her. When he came up again she said, looking at his face, "Trouble?"

"In a way. Not the way you mean, though."

As he walked back to his office, he asked abruptly, "How

much did you know about life when you were sixteen, Jill?"

"Bloody all. My Mum never told me a thing," Sergeant Peabody said with emphasis.

"I didn't mean that. I meant, what to expect from people. What was going to happen to you. How things go."

Jill Peabody said, "You have to find out for yourself, don't you? I mean, even if my Mum . . . I wouldn't have believed her, anyway. You don't stop people getting hurt, making fools of themselves, not by telling them. I got a lot of surprises after I was sixteen. I can remember that."

6

Vicky did not tell Chris of her visit to New Scotland Yard. This was not because she didn't think about it. She thought about it most of the time. It was the most important thing that had happened to her since her Mum's funeral. If the Chief Inspector was going to help her in her search, that would really be something. And he'd seemed as if he really wanted to. She could summon back to her inside ear the exact tone of his voice when he'd said, "Vicky! It's good to see you." She could see clearly the foreshortened view of his face, all nose and forehead, as he'd bent over the photograph, and the thick thatch of dark, silvered hair. She could almost taste the sweet milky coffee which the young police-woman had brought in. But she didn't want to talk about it. Not just because of not hurting Chris's feelings. She wanted to keep it secret, to herself.

Stephen, sweating over work for his "A" levels, thought about Vicky. He wondered if she'd been to see Price, and if so, whether she'd got anything useful from him. He wondered what sort of parents Vicky had sprung from, what it would be like to find a quite unknown father who might even not know you existed. He thought of the long tress of black hair. It was darker than the hair of any English girls he'd met. Perhaps Vicky's mother had come from one of the Mediterranean countries? Unlikely. Mrs. Stanford would certainly have told Vicky if her mother had been foreign. But her father might turn out to be Italian or Greek or something like that, that might mean her going to live in a distant country where he'd never see her.

He was reminded of his offer to try to discover the background of the photograph. To have something definite to tell her would be a good excuse for calling again. He took the snapshot out of the envelope he'd been keeping it in and looked again at the tiny blurred face above the rail. "I wonder if you're alive or dead? Perhaps you're Vicky's great-grandfather. Perhaps you're a hundred and fifty years old, alive and well and living in Georgia." He'd read somewhere that the Georgians were supposed to live well into their second century, remarrying and starting third or fourth families at the age of a hundred and twenty.

"Did you say something?" his mother asked. She was in the hall at the bottom of the stairs as he came out of his room on the landing above.

"I didn't mean to." He wondered if he'd spoken his thoughts aloud and was grateful it hadn't been his Dad below. That would have meant ten minutes' explanation and interpretation. He ran down the flight of stairs and held the photograph out for his mother to see. "Know where that is, Mum?"

She took it from him and looked closely.

"No. Should I? I don't remember ever seeing him before."

"Not him. I mean, not who. Where? You wouldn't ever have seen this person. I just wanted to know if you recognized the place where he is. That thing behind him."

She looked again. "Is it a bridge?" she asked.

"I think it must be. Only where?"

It was bad luck that at this moment Dr. Rawlinson let himself in at the front door and saw his wife and son studying the snapshot.

"What's that? You taking up photography, Stephen?" he asked, taking off his coat and hanging it carefully on a hanger.

Stephen said "No," and would have reclaimed the photograph, but he was too late. His mother had already put it into her husband's outstretched hand. Stephen felt the familiar slow tide of rage rising within him at the prospect of what his father was likely to say. In fact it was an innocuous question. "Hm. Friend of yours?"

Stephen made himself answer coolly. "No one any of us knows."

"So what interests you about it?" his father asked.

"I was asking Mum if she recognized the place. The background."

"We thought it might be a bridge," Mrs. Rawlinson said.

"Yes. Certainly a bridge," Dr. Rawlinson agreed.

"Any idea where, Dad?"

"It's a big drop. And that cliff... Those stratification lines..."

"What lines? I didn't see any lines," Mrs. Rawlinson said, and Stephen waited, cringing, for his father to make one of his really damaging comments. Instead of which, he said, in an almost human way, "Look, there! You can see the layers. Not horizontal, sloping. Pity it isn't a colour photograph. They'd show up more clearly."

"There can't be a lot of bridges with cliffs like that, can there?" Stephen asked.

"Not in Britain. This was taken in Britain, was it?"

Stephen's heart sank. He said, "I don't know."

"It'll take some time to sort out if you have the whole globe to choose from," Dr. Rawlinson said.

"It's a pity the trees are so far away. You could have told something by the sort they were," Mrs. Rawlinson said.

"I don't know how many suspension bridges there are in the world, but I imagine the number might run into hundreds if not..." Dr. Rawlinson was saying, but Stephen interrupted him.

"How d'you know it's a suspension bridge, Dad?"

"Because of the uprights. There, going up vertically from the bridge to the overhead chains. You can't see the chains, here, of course, but..."

"But if you're sure it's a suspension bridge, that's great! I mean, it'd be that much easier to find, than if it was just an ordinary bridge. Wouldn't it?"

"Would you like to explain why the whereabouts of this bridge is so important, Stephen?" Dr. Rawlinson said, handing back the photograph. Stephen hesitated. He was torn between the impulse to say something young and rude, and the knowledge that his father had put him a step further in the search, and that he, Stephen, was getting too old to behave like a child whenever his father irritated him. He swallowed, then said, "No, Dad. I don't really want to, and anyway it's not really anything to do with me. I was just interested because the photo belongs to a friend, who asked me if I knew where it was."

He saw his mother's look of relief and knew that she'd been expecting him to come out with something offhand, if not plain disagreeable. His father, too, reacted, but in an unexpected way. He said, almost as to an equal, "Of course. I didn't mean to intrude into your private affairs." He couldn't help speaking in that stilted way, Stephen knew. It was no good letting his own temper rise just because his father didn't talk in the ordinary language other people used. Stephen remembered his English master as school, commenting on somebody's essay, saying, "When you find a piece of writing that's unnecess-arily complicated or pompous, using twenty long words where six simple ones would do, you'll always know the writer's not sure what he really means, what he really wants to say. It's a sort of protective device." Stephen won-dered if his father's way of speaking was a protection. Not that he didn't know what he wanted to say, but perhaps that he wasn't sure how it would be received. Almost as if he was frightened. But that was ridiculous! Frightened of Mum, who curled up when he so much as looked at her? Frightened of his own son? But it occurred now to Stephen, for the first time ever, that his father's habit of taking the su-perior attitude towards his family might just possibly be compared to the behaviour of Johnny Smithers at his first school. Johnny had knocked down everyone on first meeting: not because he really wanted to make enemies, but because he was frightened that he himself would get beaten up if he didn't get in first.

It was this novel idea that made him say to his father, "Thanks, Dad," and leave the house without any further exchanges. But all the way to the library, where he was going to spend the morning working, he was absorbed in the curious notion that his Dad, in spite of being a psychiatrist, and, it seemed, a successful one, wasn't all that sure of where he stood with his own wife and son. Felt uneasy with them, had to put on a sort of act. For almost the first time that he could remember, Stephen felt something like pity for his father.

That evening, primed with his reason for calling, he rang the bell at the Stanford house. Vicky opened the door. From the kitchen beyond he heard the sounds of a television programme and said, "Am I interrupting something you're watching?"

She said, "Paul and Chris are. It's something about the way you use computers." She sounded uninterested.

"Could I come in for a minute? I've got something to tell you."

She opened the door wider. "Of course you can. We could go into the front room if it won't take long. It's not very warm there."

He followed her into the front room. It smelled cold and unused. He remembered an uncomfortable interview here with Detective Inspector Price and Vicky and himself. Vicky perched on a chair. Stephen sat on another and they faced each other, warily.

Vicky said, "What did you want to tell me?"

"About the photograph," Stephen said. He took it from his pocket and put it on the table. He said, "I showed it to my parents. I hope you don't mind."

"You didn't say . . ."

"I didn't tell them where it came from. Just said it belonged to a friend who'd asked me if I knew where it was."

She looked relieved.

"Did one of them know?"

"Not really. But my father said it must be a suspension bridge. Because of those upright things. See?" He pointed.

"I don't see how that helps," Vicky said, disappointingly cool.

"It means there aren't hundreds of thousands of bridges

48

all over the world to choose from. Only hundreds. When I started looking them up . . ."

"How d'you mean, looking them up?"

"When I was in the library this morning I tried those big encyclopaedias. They weren't any good. No pictures, mostly diagrams, and lists of bridges all over the world. I didn't think I'd ever find this one." He wanted Vicky to realize the efforts he made for her. The search in the library had taken a good hour.

"But you did? Find it, I mean?"

"I got the assistant to find me books just about bridges. There were eight of them . . . may have been nine. So I looked through for pictures that showed suspension bridges over big drops, with cliffs like in your photograph. Most of the right sort of bridges hadn't got cliffs at all, or you could see the water below them, quite near. That was in the first three of the books. Then I found one which showed a really deep drop, but the cliff the other side from where the picture was taken wasn't like in yours. I knew it just could be the right one, so in the next book I looked up its name, and it was there! A photograph taken from the other side, just like yours, with the strata lines on the cliff and that little building on top. So then I knew . . ."

"Where?" Vicky asked. He'd got all her attention now.

"It's the Clifton suspension bridge. In Bristol."

"Bristol? That's in the west country, isn't it?"

"On the Severn estuary. It's quite a big port."

"You can't see any sea in the photograph."

"The Clifton bridge doesn't go across the estuary. It goes across a sort of gorge. It's the Avon, the river, down at the bottom. One of the pictures in the book in the library showed it much better than here."

"I wonder why he got his picture taken on a bridge," Vicky said.

"It's famous. It was a new design or something. I didn't have time to read all about it . . ."

"Very famous?" Vicky said.

"What difference does that make?"

"Because if it's like the Houses of Parliament or Trafalgar

Square, people come from anywhere to look at it and get photographed there to show they've seen it."

Stephen saw that she was right. In self-defence, he said, "You might do that if you were living there yourself, but your friends weren't."

"I suppose so." Neither of them said what they were both thinking, that a young man might well send an absent girl-friend this sort of snapshot. Vicky said, with more warmth, "It was really nice of you to find out for me, Stephen. Thanks a lot."

"Did you find out anything?" Stephen asked.

"I went to the hospital like you said."

Stephen's mind was far away. He said, "The hospital. What for?"

"You said to see if anyone there remembered my mother."

"Did you find anyone who did?"

"I couldn't find anybody at first. I mean, they were all porters and receptionists."

"No good then?"

"Yes. Well. Better than nothing. But the nurses . . . they were so young. Not that much older than me."

"What about the doctors?" Stephen asked.

"I couldn't think of a good reason for getting to see one. You know how they are in hospitals. They all looked . . . sort of . . . busy."

Stephen knew exactly what she meant.

"And it wasn't visiting hours. I hadn't worked it out properly, I suppose. There wasn't anyone to talk to. Except the Sister."

"You talked to the Sister!" Stephen was amazed. When he'd been in hospital for his appendix, four years before, the Sister had been a terrifying figure in a tight blue dress, at whose nod everyone had trembled. The doctors too.

"I felt such a fool. After going all that way and then not getting to speak to anyone. So I walked into her office," Vicky was saying.

"What was she like?" Stephen asked.

"Frightening. Especially at the beginning. But she did let

50

me explain . . ."

"Did she remember your mother?"

"She got nicer after I'd said . . . She'd been a midwife on the ward then. A student midwife, she said."

"Had she looked after your mother?" Stephen asked.

"No, it wasn't her. It was another of the midwives. But she did remember my mother dying, and Mum taking the two of us home with her."

"Wasn't it any use at all, then?"

"It might be. Well, I don't know. Yet," Vicky said.

"What do you mean?"

"She gave me the name of the other one. Another midwife who did look after my mother."

"So what? Would she remember anything?"

"She might. Anyway I'm going to try."

"Try what?"

"Going to see her. I've got her address, and her name. She's married. I shall go and ask," Vicky said, defiant.

"Where does she live?" Stephen asked. If it was far away, right up in the north of the country, or west, like Bristol, Vicky might like him to go with her. At least he'd be there to support her if all she met was disappointment. He was disappointed himself when Vicky said, "South London. I'm going to see her as soon as I can without having to tell Chris."

"Did you go and see Price, too?"

"Yes."

"No good?" Stephen asked, prepared to sympathize again.

"He says no one's going to help me till I'm eighteen. It's the law."

"Is that all? Wasn't he . . . friendly? He used to be all right. I quite liked him."

"He is all right. He's great." It was clear that she didn't mean to say any more about what Stephen thought must have been a hurtful failure. He said, longing to comfort her, "I wish there was something I could do."

"There isn't anything anyone can. But it's really nice of you to want to help."

Emboldened by this, Stephen said, "Vicky!"

"What?"

"I know you don't like it, but I thought ... if there wasn't anything else ... I brought my bits of the Egg ..." He tumbled them out of the plastic bag in which they were kept, on the table.

Vicky looked at the scattered pieces of wood. Little crooked shapes. They made no sense, lying there higgledy-piggledy. Who would ever have guessed that when they were fitted together in their own intricate, interlocking pattern, they would add up to a whole, smoothly polished wooden Egg? Not that she'd ever seen it like that for more than the split second when Stephen had put it together, his many pieces and the one odd one which she'd found by chance. They had believed that this bit was the only one wanting to restore the Egg to its original complete, secure egg shape. But hers hadn't been the only missing fragment, and when Stephen's fingers had relaxed their hold, the Egg had fallen again into meaningless particles. But even in its incomplete state, it had been the Egg which had imposed those flashes of vision of future events which Vicky and Stephen had unwillingly shared. Stephen was inviting her to test this power again now.

She said, "No."

"It mightn't work, but if there's nothing else, wouldn't it be worth trying?"

"You didn't like it any more than I did," Vicky said.

"I'd do it if you wanted," Stephen said.

Vicky looked again at the fragmented Egg. For a moment Stephen thought she was going to agree. Instead she shivered. She said, "It's cold in here," and he realized that she was dismissing the idea. He shovelled the wooden shapes back into the plastic bag and pocketed it. Stood up. Vicky picked up the photograph and stood up too.

"I'm sorry, Stephen. You've been great about it, but I can't. Even if it was the only way. And anyhow ... I just know it wouldn't work."

"It's all right. You don't have to be sorry about anything."

At the front door she said, "Sometimes I think I might as well not go on trying. I don't believe I'll ever know anything about who I really am."

With unusual conviction, Stephen found he was saying, "You will."

"You're just saying that."

But with the assurance he had once drawn from those transient flashes of vision from the rejected Egg, Stephen repeated, "You will. You'll find out what you want. Some time or other. I'm not just saying it, I'm sure."

Vicky rewarded him with a warmer look than she'd given him all through the evening. But as he walked home, Stephen's thoughts were gloomy. His great discovery of the whereabouts of the bridge hadn't been the triumph he'd hoped for, and she'd refused the only other method of help he had to offer. If he'd proved that her father had come from the other side of the world and she had set off to look for him, she could hardly have been further removed from him than she was in her present mood.

There were some things, Price thought, you never got used to. Years of dealing with crime of all kinds, violence, murder, the lot, hadn't made him immune to this sort of story. It was always when it was something to do with a kid, that he found himself getting emotionally involved, not keeping the cool, reasoned approach which was right and effective. The fact that this time it was an unattractive kid whom nobody liked or wanted, didn't make any difference. She'd run away from home half a dozen times before and come back again, generally half-starved. God knew what horrible things she'd discovered on those abortive escapades, which had made her miserable home seem the better alternative. This last time, her parents didn't trouble to inform the police. They'd presumably expected the bad penny to turn up again. Well, she had turned up. Assaulted and battered to death in a small wood on the outskirts of London. She was fifteen, an age at which other girls were just leaving behind them reasonably happy, secure childhoods and were preparing to become reasonably happy, balanced young women.

Like Vicky.

It was two weeks since Vicky had come here to see him, and he hadn't done anything, hadn't even thought of what he might do. It wasn't that he had forgotten her; he'd thought of her more than once, with a sort of compassionate affection, but he'd hardly spared a moment to consider her problem. He'd been busy, yes. But that was normal, there was never a day when he didn't have pressing questions to be dealt with. He knew that it was because he hadn't felt confident of ever being able to do anything that might really help that he had stored the subject away in a pigeon-hole in his mind, labelled "to be dealt with later", like the letters to which there was no easy reply, which got shelved indefinitely. Now, thinking about the wretched Tracy's life and horrible end, he thought of his promise to Vicky that he'd let her know if he could think of any likely trail to follow. Putting it to the back of his mind wasn't exactly what she'd expect from him.

Tracy's story had jolted his memory of Vicky. Now it gave him an idea. He picked up the telephone and rang through to the room where the Index of Missing Persons was kept.

"Danny? Jim Price here. Could you do something for me?"

"Tell me what you want and I'll tell ye if I'll do it."

"I'd like you to look up a girl who went missing seventeen, maybe eighteen years ago. Might have been more."

"Tell me about her," said Danny's agreeable, Irish voice.

"That's the trouble, I don't know much. She was young. Probably about seventeen, eighteen. Something like that. Dark hair. Probably had some education. But working class." He was trying to remember the odd facts that he'd gleaned from Vicky's conversation when she'd come to see him here. She'd told him about the black hair and Mrs. Stanford's summing up of the girl's background, as they'd gone down in the lift together. It added up to very little, and he wasn't surprised to hear Danny's snort of disgust.

"And where might this young chick have come from? I presume you know that?" Danny asked.

"Not a ghost of an idea," Price said cheerfully.

"Married, was she?"

"Not married. May have been pregnant."

"Do you happen to know for certain she was reported missing at all?"

"No, Danny, I don't know that."

"And that's all you want for me to be finding out for ye?" with heavy irony.

"I know there must have been hundreds . . ."

"Hundreds? Man, there's thousands. Do you know how many girls not yet turned seventeen go missing each year? And you're asking me to find one black-haired damsel for ye out of all that number? You don't know her age, you don't know where she'd have come from, you don't know which year it was, or whether she'd have been reported missing in the first place. Is that the sort of question to be asking from a friend?" The receiver was jammed down. Price almost laughed aloud. He knew his Danny. But then he frowned. It looked as if he wouldn't have anything to tell Vicky, except that he'd tried and failed.

While he was thinking this, Vicky was on her way to try to find Mrs. Banks, who had once been Nurse Betty Turner. Her address was Sixteen, Nossiter Terrace. It was in Dulwich, a long way from Hampstead. Vicky had searched in the A to Z in the library, when she was supposed to be reading for her exams, and had worked out how to get there. Tube and then bus. It would take ages.

She'd have liked to escape from the house without having to say where she was going. But Chris was working mostly at home, and it seemed easiest, if not entirely truthful, to say, "I'm going to the library. Coming?"

"No. I've got masses to do here. Besides, it's Dad's late shift. He'll want dinner."

Vicky's conscience pricked her. She'd forgotten.

"Shal I stay, then?"

"Course not. But won't you be back?"

"I might not come back till afternoon. I can always go out and get a Wimpy or something if I haven't finished."

Guilt made Vicky believe that Chris saw through her pretence. But she didn't say any more and Vicky left the house carrying her book-bag, without having to answer any more questions. She went first to the library, partly to salve her conscience, partly to deposit the books with the friendly girl at the desk. Lightened in body if not in mind, Vicky started off on her journey.

It took nearly two hours to reach Dulwich. The buses were infrequent and the conductor didn't tell her where to get off, so she overshot her mark and had to walk back. Although she'd memorized the way to Nossiter Terrace, the actual lay-out of the streets was not as simple as it had looked on the map. She had to ask for directions more than once, and wasn't always helped by what she was told. When at last she reached the road it was after midday. She'd left home before half-past nine. It would certainly be mid-afternoon before she was back.

Nossiter Terrace was made up of small houses, built of red brick with white stone facings. Originally all identical, they had responded, during their sixty years or so of survival, to very different treatments. Some had shiny new paint on their doors and window frames, and had tidy front gardens and neat curtains. Other gardens were overgrown with rank grass, and the little houses were grimy, with scuffed and peeling paint; the curtains, too, inside the dingy glass of the windows, were faded and grey.

Number sixteen was outstandingly trim. Clipped privet hedge, flagged front garden, polished knocker, glittering panes. Spotless curtains, symmetrically draped. From the other side of the immaculate front door, rose the whine of a vacuum cleaner. Vicky pressed the bell push and heard chimes.

The vacuum's whine ran down the scale and ceased. The door was opened smartly, giving the impression of impatience.

The woman who confronted Vicky was tall and slim. She wore a checked overall and a matching cotton square held back her hair. In spite of this, she managed to look elegant. Her hands, on which she wore rubber gloves, rested on the handle of the cleaner, and she said, "Yes?" in a tone which was as good as an instant dismissal.

Vicky swallowed. She said, "Mrs. Banks?"

"That's right."

"The Sister at St. Clare's gave me your name. She said you might be able to help me." Vicky had rehearsed this opening on the long trail to the house, but as it came out now it sounded less assured and less explicit than she'd hoped.

57

"Which Sister?" the woman asked.

"The Sister in the maternity ward." Vicky realized now, too late, that she hadn't asked the Sister's name.

"Sister Harris," Mrs. Banks said.

"She said you and she were pupil midwives there a long time ago."

"Well?" Mrs. Banks didn't seem anxious to help. Her fingers moved towards the switch of the cleaner, as if she was itching to get back to work.

"I was born there. The Sister thought you looked after my mother," Vicky said.

The woman looked over Vicky uncuriously. She said, "How would I know? You don't expect me to remember..."

"My mother died," Vicky said flatly.

She saw that this had thrown Mrs. Banks for the moment. She went on, "I thought perhaps you'd remember that because not many people die having babies now."

"What did she die of?" Mrs. Banks asked.

"I don't know exactly. I think it was bleeding ... sort of..."

"Sorry. Can't help," Mrs. Banks said, not sounding or looking sorry.

"I thought you might remember ... the Sister did. Because of my being adopted. By ... Mrs. Stanford in the next bed had a baby the same day. She took both of us home." Vicky hated what she was having to do. Spilling her private history out to this hostile stranger.

But it was clear that this last piece of information had penetrated. The bored expression on the woman's face changed very slightly. Her fingers left the switch of the cleaner and she said, "Yes. That's right."

"You do remember?" Vicky said.

"I remember there being a fuss because no one knew anything about the mother. No relatives. They didn't know who to contact about the baby." She spoke as if Vicky wasn't present, or had not been that small, abandoned baby.

"Please! Couldn't you tell me something about her?" Vicky urged.

58

"I think she was one of mine. I did the delivery. Straight-forward labour as far as I can remember," Mrs. Banks said, professionally.

"But . . . what was she like? My mother. Anything . . ." Vicky said, desperate.

"You don't get to know patients in the labour ward."

"But afterwards. She might have said something. Told you something about herself," Vicky suggested. But she already knew that it was a hopeless quest. Impossible to imagine this woman inviting confidence of any sort.

"You're busy when you're doing Midder. Looking after two patients for every bed. The baby as well as the mother. Sorry, can't help you," Mrs. Banks said. She eased the rubber gloves further over her fingers to indicate that she had spent all the time she meant to spare on this useless exchange.

Vicky said, "I see. Thanks." She had taken a step back from the open door when, in a last attempt, she said, "If you did remember anything, would you let me know?"

Mrs. Banks said, "I don't suppose I shall. Not likely." Her tone told Vicky that she didn't mean to expend any energy on trying.

"But if you did. *Please!*"

"All right." Ungraciously.

She'd never bother to write. Vicky thought quickly. "I'll give you my name and the number where you could leave a message." She'd have to warn Stephen. A bit unfair to use him like this, but she must. She found a biro and a scruffy bit of paper, the other side of an envelope that had already been used as a shopping list. She wrote her name and Stephen Rawlinson's telephone number and held it out towards Mrs. Banks.

"There just might be something," she said.

Mrs. Banks glanced at the paper and put it in the pocket of her overall. She said, "Bye-bye" and shut the door before Vicky was off the step. As she walked down the flagged path Vicky heard the crescendo of the vacuum cleaner start up again, Mrs. Banks had already dismissed the matter from her mind.

8

When Vicky got back, late in the afternoon, Chris was in the kitchen with her hands in a mixing bowl. She was angry.

"Where've you *been*? You said the library!" she accused.

"I did... Oh hell! I've left all my books there!" Vicky said.

"The girl at the desk said you left them there at half nine and she hadn't seen you since. I've been worried sick. I rang Stephen..."

"You didn't!" Vicky realized that Chris must indeed have been frantic. She said, "I'm sorry. I thought I'd be back for dinner, but it was miles away and the buses seemed never to come when I wanted." She was tired and miserable. It was almost too much to be greeted like this.

"Where did you go?"

"Dulwich."

"*Dulwich*! What on earth for?"

It wasn't any good trying to keep it secret. Vicky told her. Briefly, trying not to show how much she minded the failure of the futile journey. Chris didn't stop beating the butter and sugar, stirring in the flour, breaking the eggs, but she listened. At the end, when Vicky was dreading the reaction of hurt feelings, Chris surprised her by saying nicely, "Poor you."

"You don't...? I mean, don't you mind?"

"I'm not keen. You know that. But I do see you've got to try."

"That wasn't what you said before."

"I talked about it to Paul. He said he'd feel the same if it was him. He'd try to find out where he came from."

Vicky could have cried with relief. Even knowing that Chris had discussed her problems with Paul didn't spoil it. She shut her eyes against tears and heard Chris's voice saying, "You look terrible. Didn't you have any dinner?"

Vicky shook her head, dumb. She heard movements, the tap running, the "plop" of the gas lighting up, the door of the fridge being opened and shut. It was wonderful just to sit in the warm kitchen and to let someone else take decisions and act for her. She smelled toast. The water in the kettle settled down to the quiet hum of boiling. When she opened her eyes there was a plate of hot buttered toast on the table by her, and a cup of milky coffee.

"Go on, eat something. You'll feel a lot better," Chris said. She sounded like her mother: comforting, safe. Vicky ate the toast and drank the coffee. Chris poured the cake mixture into a tin and put it in the oven.

"Mum's chocolate coffee cake. I had to do something. I couldn't read," she said, and added, as she took the bowl and spoons over to the sink to wash, "Funny how being anxious makes you cross. Mum used to be, when we got home late, didn't she?"

"I'm really sorry. I couldn't let you know."

"Paul says we'll have to go on the phone some time."

"Dad won't. Ever," Vicky said.

"I don't know. If we start staying out late and we can't let him know, he might."

"Could I have some more coffee?" Vicky asked. She was feeling a lot better. Even the sore resentment that Mrs. Banks's attitude had aroused was fading in the comfort of Chris's solicitude. As Chris filled her cup again, she said, "What did you say to Stephen?"

"Just asked him if he'd seen you. I think he got worried too. He might come round this evening to see if you're all right."

"I'll have to get back to the library to get my books before it shuts," Vicky said.

"You've got plenty of time. It's not five yet. Don't fuss," Chris said.

In Dulwich, Mrs. Banks had completed her day's programme of spring cleaning. The paint in the kitchen was washed down, the store cupboards turned out, the curtains, which she'd taken down and put in the machine that morning, were just ready for a nice iron. She should now have felt relaxed, with a gratified pride in her virtuous fatigue.

Instead, for no reason she could make out, she was uneasy. Generally this would have meant that she had overlooked some corner where dirt might be collecting, or that she'd forgotten to turn off the switch of the washing machine or to adjust the clock on the boiler. But when she had checked and double checked, and had found nothing left undone, the niggling irritation at the back of her mind still persisted.

It was there all through tea and the silly chatter of the two kids. It was there while she smoothed out the freshly laundered curtains, a job she usually enjoyed. She tried to pin it down, to think of what she'd already accomplished and of what she would do tomorrow, but instead of seeing the glistening tidiness of her home, the picture that came before her mind's eye was the face of the girl who'd come bothering her in the middle of her work that morning.

At the same time, she remembered something Megan had said at tea. Megan, aged twelve, was a sensible girl, only apt to be soppy sometimes about people she liked. There was a new young teacher at her school just now that she was keen on, and she'd said about her, "She's a lovely person." Lovely! A stupid way to talk about a quite ordinary young woman. Betty Banks had told Megan what she thought about silly talk like that, and Megan had shut up, like a clam.

The pricking itch of something half remembered grew suddenly more demanding. In spite of her determination to dismiss it, it wouldn't let her rest. She could feel, as if it were a creature clambering up to the light from a deep,

deep pool, the memory of something she'd heard, making its way up from the depths of years past, to the surface of her mind. Like an echo, she heard another voice, not Megan's, saying, "She's a lovely person." And again, she felt her own annoyance at the stupid enthusiasm of the speaker, and she heard her own sharp reply. "She'll need to be more than that if she's going to look after two kids the same age, at her time of life!"

The memory flooded back, like the picture on a screen. That stupid little probationer, Sue Stickley, always going off the deep end about something or other, and the woman they'd been talking about. Late thirties, had had a difficult time with her first baby, now sitting there, grinning all over her fat face, in the nursery for premature infants, holding two babies, one on each arm. Talking silly to both of them. One of those babies must've been the plain girl with the straight hair who'd come to the door today.

Well! A lot of help that was! No need to ring up anyone to say that she remembered Sue Stickley talking. She'd always been talking. Spent half her time gossiping with the patients instead of getting on with the proper business of nursing. That same time she'd been on about the lovely woman, she'd been talking about another patient. She'd said, "Real black her hair was. Almost like Spanish." She'd said, "Back near my home, people tell that when those ships came over from Spain to fight Good Queen Bess, some of them were wrecked on our rocks and the sailors that got off alive settled in the country. Married Cornish girls, and that's maybe where the black hair comes from." Betty Banks hadn't time for these old tales. She'd said, "She probably lived in London all her life." And Sue had said, "No, she's Cornish. I'd know her voice anywhere. Makes me feel like at home."

Betty Banks shook out the curtains and before supper she'd got them back up on their runners. As she laid the table for supper, she tried to dismiss the whole subject from her mind. What good would it do that stupid girl to hear gossip like this? Sue was such a tattler, she'd probably got her patients mixed up. Betty Banks couldn't be sure it had been the girl who'd died that Sue had been talking about.

She did her best to forget it. After supper, when she'd done the dishes and said goodnight to the kids, she sat down in front of the television and tried to concentrate on the screen.

But this time her strong will couldn't suppress the nagging voice that told her what she should do. At half past nine, after she'd heard the news, she felt in the pocket of her overall, hanging on its hook in the kitchen, and went out into the hall, and picked up the telephone receiver.

It was that evening, just before ten o'clock, that Stephen rang the bell at the Stanfords' door.

Chris opened it. Stephen asked at once, "Is she back?"

"Oh! I'm sorry, Steve! I ought've let you know. She got back this afternoon. She's been..." She hesitated, not sure how much Stephen already knew. "She's been to Dulwich to see someone."

"I know. I've got a message for her. Can I see her?"

"We're in the kitchen. Paul's here too," Chris said, leading the way.

Stephen saw Vicky and Paul sitting at the table. He saw at once that Vicky was exhausted and miserable. She looked wan. Paul said, "Hi!" and made room for Stephen to sit beside him, opposite to Vicky. She hardly raised her eyes to look at him.

Chris was at the cooker, boiling water for another of the endless cups of tea or coffee he'd already drunk in that room. Stephen was trying to make up his mind whether this was the moment to give Vicky the message which had brought him there, when Paul said, "Haven't seen you for months."

"You and Chris were watching a programme about computers last time I came round. I wouldn't have understood a word," Stephen said.

"That's right. You would have, though. It wasn't for specialists. For the general public. The intelligent ones, of course," Paul said, with a sudden, surprisingly sweet smile.

"Next time I'll try," Stephen said. Chris, coming back to the table with the cup – it was coffee this time – said, "I understood a lot of it, didn't I?"

"You said you did." He smiled at Chris too, and Stephen thought, "I wish Vicky and I were like they are. Sure about each other."

"You working very hard?" Paul asked Stephen.

"Trying to. It's not easy at home."

"Do your parents think you're overworking if you stay in your room for more than an hour or two? Mine used to," Paul said.

"Not exactly. It's more like feeling they're watching all the time. When I come out of my room, I can feel my mother hovering. She wants to ask how I'm getting on, but she doesn't like to, so she says things like, wouldn't I like supper early, or morning coffee, or something like that."

"My Mum's a bit like that. She used to fry onions and leave the kitchen door open. She thought when I smelled them, I'd have to come down and eat," Paul said.

"And did you?" Chris asked.

"When I got hungry. Not as much as my Mum'd have liked. It's funny. I think it's something to do with having kids, makes women think getting food into you is going to make everything better," Paul said.

"That's right! When one of us was upset about anything, the first thing Mum always did was to make cups of tea and hand out the biscuits," Chris said.

"It does raise your blood sugar," Stephen said. Then he felt that he must have sounded pompous, over-scientific. He was grateful to Vicky for saying, "They do make you feel better, often."

"What would your Dad say about Mums wanting to feed their kids?" Chris asked Stephen, teasing. She'd always enjoyed Stephen's accounts of his Dad's elaborate psychological explanations of the most ordinary behaviour.

His Dad would have said a lot, Stephen thought. Had said a lot, indeed, and much of it he wasn't going to repeat.

65

He said, "He thinks my mother's *thing* about cooking . . . you know she's always trying out new things . . . My father thinks that's where all her creative energy goes to. Sort of trying to be as good as a man." It sounded stupid and he wasn't surprised that Chris pounced.

"That's silly! Your Mum doesn't have to try anything like that. I think she just enjoys cooking, like I do. Vicky does, too, and Mum did. She wasn't trying to be as good as anyone else."

Stephen saw Paul put a hand, unobtrusively, on Chris's arm. Paul said, "I don't think it's like that. It's something to do with looking after babies . . ."

"Babies! What . . . ?" Chris began.

"Feeding them. You know. It's mothers that do that, isn't it? To keep them alive, and comforted, and all that. So when their kids grow up, that's the first thing they think of when they want to help."

Stephen thought, "That's common sense." He thought of the words his own father would have employed on the subject, and wondered, as he had before, if his Dad didn't perhaps retreat into jargon when he was talking to his own family, in order to hide the fact that although he thought he *knew* about people, he didn't trust his feelings about them. He had a sudden rush of pity. Poor Dad! How terrible to be so . . . *constipated* with the two persons nearest to him.

"Does your Dad watch like you said your Mum does?" Chris was asking him, and Stephen found himself able to laugh as he said, "He keeps on telling me he's not going to ask anything, and then he waits for me to talk. It's terrible."

"That's the psycho-analytic technique, isn't it? You don't ask, you let the patient come out with whatever's bothering him," Paul said.

"That's right. Only I'm not a patient. Not yet. I daresay I will be if Dad hangs around being expectant like that till I've finished with the exams."

"Our Dad doesn't watch to see if we're working, thank goodness," Chris said comfortably.

"He doesn't need to worry. You've both of you been working really hard," Paul said.

66

"Sometimes we have. Only there's such a lot of other things. Shopping and cooking and horrible housework," Chris said.

Of course! Stephen hadn't thought before of the extra burden that must fall on the two girls as a result of their Mum's death. If he'd been alone with Vicky he might have spoken his startled sympathy aloud. Almost as if he had read this thought, Paul pushed his cup away from him and stood up. "I'll have to be going. Have to get up early in the morning."

"Your term started?" Stephen asked.

"Tomorrow. 'Bye. Good luck with your 'A's. 'Bye, Vicky." He went towards the door, followed by Chris.

When they had gone, Stephen said to Vicky, still sitting listless in her chair, "I came round because I've got a message for you."

She did look at him then, startled, with big eyes. "She rang you?"

"A woman. She said she was Mrs. Banks. About half an hour ago. No, more like three quarters."

"I'm sorry! I meant to tell you . . . I had to give her your number because of us not being on the phone." Vicky was crimson with embarrassment.

"That's all right. It was me that answered, so it wasn't as if Dad took the call and thought she was a patient," Stephen said.

"The thing was, I never thought she would. She didn't seem as if she meant to try to think of anything. What did she say?" Vicky asked, eager now.

"Said she'd remembered some nurse who'd been in the hospital with her . . . Said this other nurse had looked after your mother. This other nurse thought your mother came from the same part of the country as she did. She was Cornish, and she thought your mother talked like the people round where she came from. Or somewhere near," Stephen said, confusedly.

"Where did she come from? The other nurse? Where in Cornwall?"

"She didn't know. The Banks woman. At least, she

didn't say. She seemed in a hurry and ... sort of cross,"
Stephen said.

"She was like that when I saw her too."

There was a silence. Chris reappeared at the door and
came over to the table.

"I was telling Vicky. The woman in Dulwich rang me this
evening. She'd remembered that one of the other nurses
thought Vicky's mother came from Cornwall," Stephen
said.

"Why didn't she tell me when I was there?" Vicky said in
a small, cold voice.

"She said she'd only just remembered."

"Will it help?" Chris asked. Vicky didn't answer.
Stephen, disappointed, said, "I thought you'd want to
know as soon as you could."

"Yes. Thanks."

"But just Cornwall! How could you start looking all over
Cornwall, when you don't even know the name for
certain?" Chris asked.

Vicky said, "I don't know. I suppose it'd be somewhere
to start." Her voice was anything but hopeful.

There didn't seem anything worth waiting for. Stephen
stood up. "I'd better go. I've got mountains of work."

Chris looked at Vicky. Her responsibility. Vicky knew it.
She went with Stephen out of the kitchen to the front door.

"Vicky?" he said, as she laid her hand on the latch.

With an effort, she said, "Thanks, Stephen. It was nice of
you to come round so quickly."

She knew she was disappointing him, but she was too
tired, too fed up to feel the enthusiasm he deserved. She
shut the door behind him feeling bad. He had been kind
and she had been ungracious. But Chris was right. This
tiny item of information didn't promise to get her much
further in her search.

9

The next morning Vicky went again to the library, and this time she stayed there. But on her way back for lunch she went into the public call box near the shops. She had been here ages ago with Stephen and then they'd been trying to speak to the same person that she was asking for now. But it felt entirely different. Then they'd been tense and anxious about the kidnapped baby whose whereabouts Price was trying to pinpoint, time had been short, every clue she and Stephen could provide was important. Now there was no urgency, and the quest she was on was a matter entirely her own. It wouldn't matter to anyone else if she succeeded. Nor if she failed.

The telephone in Chief Detective Inspector Price's office rang and he picked up the receiver impatiently.

"It's a Miss Stanford, sir, asking to speak to you," the girl on the switchboard said.

"Put her through."

There were the routine clicks and then he heard Vicky's voice, trembling slightly.

"Is that Superintendent Price?"

"That's right. It's Vicky, isn't it?"

"Yes, it's me."

"If you're ringing to ask if I've come up with any brilliant ideas, I'm afraid the answer is, No. I haven't."

She didn't sound too much deflated as she said, "No, it wasn't really that. I just thought I ought to tell you something."

"What's that?" Price asked, apprehensive, he wasn't sure why.

"I went to see someone who used to be a nurse. A midwife. I mean, she was a midwife at the hospital where I was born . . ."

Price's heart sank. He'd had plenty of experience with people who "remembered" long after the event. It wasn't in human nature, he knew, to admit that they had nothing to say. And the stories he'd heard! When they'd repeated them a couple of times the tellers themselves believed those stories and the circumstantial details came thronging in. He didn't want Vicky to be exposed to anything like that.

"She hardly told me anything. She said nurses didn't remember their patients," he heard Vicky say.

He wondered why she had taken the trouble to ring him to tell him this. He said, cautiously, "Nothing that was any help?"

"I don't know. She said she didn't remember, but then afterwards . . ."

"Afterwards?" he prompted.

"I'd left her Stephen's number. Because of us not being on the phone." Vicky must have picked up his bewilderment at this apparently unrelated remark, because she said, breathless, "I'm sorry! I'm explaining terribly badly."

Price said, "Don't worry. Take your time. Did she ring Stephen, then?"

"Yes. That same evening. Yesterday. She told him there'd been another nurse who'd talked about my . . . my mother."

"Talked to the woman you went to see, you mean?" It was all going to be the worst sort of third-hand evidence.

"That's right. She'd said she thought my mother came from the West Country. Cornwall, probably. Because she was Cornish herself. This other nurse was. So she sort of recognized the way she talked."

Price made himself say, as heartily as he could, "Well! That's something to start with."

"There's a lot of Cornwall, isn't there?" Vicky's voice sounded dispirited.

Price thought quickly. He didn't want to tell her how her piece of information might fit in with the way he'd been thinking. No point in raising hopes which were almost certain to be dashed. The chances of finding Jenny Morgan's family, even with the knowledge of the county she'd come from, were small.

"I'm amazed that you've got so far so quickly," he said.

"Will it help? Really?"

Price chose his words with care. "It's difficult to say that it's going to be much help. But it's a sort of lead. If we ever get round to doing a proper search, at least we'd know where to begin."

Such a long silence followed this remark, that he said into the phone, "Vicky?"

"Yes."

"What are you thinking?"

"I was thinking . . . You said 'We'. Do you mean you are going to help? I didn't think . . ."

He must be extra careful now. "I'm sorry. I'm so used to talking like a policeman, I do it when I'm being a private person too. I can't undertake an official search, you know. That doesn't come within my . . . It's not something the police are here for. I meant you and I . . . not me as a policeman, but as your friend. Perhaps I should say as someone who hopes that you'll find . . ." It was too difficult and he couldn't finish the sentence. He didn't really want her to go off on this wild-goose-chase, which he thought couldn't bring her anything but disappointment. What did he hope she'd find? Happiness? Peace of mind, perhaps. But those were things one didn't say.

Vicky seemed not to have noticed his uncertainty. Her voice was jubilant. "That's stupe of you! Thanks terribly . . ."

"That's *what*?" Price asked.

"Stupe. Stupendous. It's silly. It's what people at school say. Sorry. I should have said it's very kind." There was a touching dignity in the voice.

"Don't be sorry. Why should I mind being stupendous? I'm afraid you're the only person likely to think so."

71

The other telephone on his desk shrilled, making him jump.

"Yes? Yes. Hold on a moment, I'm on the other line." Back to Vicky, "I'll have to ring off now, I'm wanted. But let me know what's happening, will you?"

He was surprised at the fervour with which she said, "Thanks thousands. I'll tell you if there's anything else. Bye."

"Bye. Look after yourself," Price said, and rang off. What a nice child she was. He felt warmed by her enthusiasm. Having dealt with the other call – dreary routine stuff, – he rang Danny again.

"I know. You'd like me to be looking for the fish that got away twenty years ago in the trout stream you were poaching and you no bigger than a wheat stalk," Danny said immediately.

"Nearly right."

"It's not that girl you're still after? The one with the black hair? You should be ashamed of yourself. You're no better than a dirty old . . ."

"She came from the West Country, possibly Cornwall," Price said and cut the line on Danny's Irish blasphemies.

10

The summer term began with a flurry of agitated instructions from anxious teachers.

"You'd think no one had ever taken exams before," Chris said.

"They ought to be used to it. They've been doing the same thing every summer for years," Vicky agreed.

"I've a good mind not to take the horrible things," Chris said.

"You must! What about your course at the Tech.?"

"I don't know. I'm not all that keen."

"I thought you wanted to do the thing with kids, even if you didn't want to do the secretarial," Vicky said.

"I'm keen on leaving school. I don't have to have five 'O' levels to do that," Chris said, truly.

The days grew longer and the time for revision shorter. Several of the teachers seemed only now to have discovered great gaps in the required knowledge, and new chunks of information were suddenly pushed at their pupils, with desperate injunctions to be sure to absorb these before the dreaded day.

"I feel like one of those geese that get force-fed," Chris complained.

"If anything more goes into my head, it's going to come out at my ears. So why try?" Vicky agreed. There wasn't time for her to think for more than five minutes about anything except school work. Only occasionally, when her anxiety woke her in the light small hours of early summer, did she have a moment to spend on thinking about her search, and to wonder what Detective Superintendent Price was doing or was going to do.

The time for the examinations came, and went past extraordinarily quickly. It seemed that one day Vicky and Chris were going to school, pale with apprehension and laden with all the special pens, pencils, rulers, india-rubbers, cough lozenges and other necessary objects. Then, a day or a decade later, they came out of their last exam into the first really hot day of the year, and went home lightened of the burden of learning and free to do anything in the world they wanted.

"I can't really believe we've finished!" Vicky said.

"How shall we celebrate?" Chris asked.

"Dunno. Go to the pictures? There's a Marx Brothers on at the Everyman." This was one of their local cinemas.

"I don't think they're as funny as they're meant to be. Anyway, I think Paul'll be coming round this evening."

"His term can't have finished yet?"

"No. He's coming down specially. Because of it being my last day."

"Is he taking you out?" Vicky asked.

"I thought perhaps we'd get some take-away food and have it here. Like Chinese. Or a curry."

"Go on," Vicky said.

"Go on what about?"

"You sounded as if you were going to say something else, and then you stopped."

"I was going to say, why don't you ask Stephen? Paul likes him a lot. It'd be nice. The four of us."

Vicky had said, "No, I don't think so," before she'd realized she was going to speak.

"Don't you like him any more?" Chris asked.

"He's all right."

"He fancies you. I can tell by the way he looks at you." Silence from Vicky.

"I thought you used to fancy him," Chris said.

"I like him all right."

"Not as much as you did?"

74

"I don't fancy him the way you mean," Vicky said, uncomfortable.

"I'm sorry. I thought it'd be fun for the four of us to go about together in the holidays."

Vicky drew an invisible doodle with one finger on the table.

"Not if you don't want," Chris said.

"Chris! Don't you see? If we all go around like you want, it'll look as if him and me are the same as you and Paul. He'll think so. Stephen."

"Mm. Suppose it would. It's a pity, though."

"I can't help how I feel," Vicky said.

"I'm sorry for Stephen, though. He isn't any different, is he? It's you that's changed." She didn't say, "It's to do with your looking for your other family", but Vicky felt the thought unspoken between them. She picked up her school bag from the floor and turned it upside down on the table.

"I'm going to get rid of everything to do with exams."

"All right, I will too. Look, let's put our rulers across between us, then I'll have this half and you can have that."

The kitchen table looked like the preparations for a small jumble sale. They stacked pencils, coloured pens, biros into boxes and threw away last-minute notes, jotted down on scraps of paper, lists of dates, principal exports of towns and countries. Notebooks, into which they'd copied the condensed knowledge by which their teachers had hoped to force them through the narrow door which led to success – a pass instead of failure – were put on one side by Vicky, thrown out by Chris. "What's the use? I'm never going to take them again, even if I've failed the lot," she said, when Vicky exclaimed at her ruthlessness.

"You won't have. Failed, I mean. But . . ."

"I don't care. Funny how you always get fluff at the bottom of bags. Can't think where it comes from," Chris said, examining the inside of her bag with disapproval.

"You took Stucco!" Vicky said, picking from Chris's side of the table a small dilapidated teddy bear, his coat worn bare, and with only one boot-button eye.

"I've always taken him whenever there was anything important. After all, it couldn't hurt."

"I'd forgotten how having just the one eye made him look ... I don't know. Sort of wicked. As if he knew a secret he wasn't going to tell." Indeed, Stucco, covered with the fluff from the bag, and shaky at his seams, had a distinctly raffish look.

"Will you take him if you go for an interview at the Tech.?" Vicky asked.

"In my pocket. Not so that anyone can see." Chris took Stucco back and looked at the still considerable spread of Vicky's possessions. She pounced suddenly, and held up the small, oddly shaped spillikin of wood.

"You can't say anything about Stucco! That's your piece of the Egg!"

"I know it's silly ..." Vicky began.

"No, it's like me. You don't really believe it'll help, but it can't hurt, and it just might make a difference."

"That's right." Vicky held out her hand for the piece of wood, but Chris was holding it in her hand, turning it this way and that.

"Vicky?"

"What?"

"Is it because of that happening to you and Stephen, with the Egg and all that? Is that why you don't want to see him now? I mean, are you afraid it might start all over again?" Chris asked.

"Don't think so." But was this why she kept this fragment of the Egg upstairs, enclosed in the silver foil? She hadn't taken it around with her once since the end of the story of the kidnapped baby, until these last days of the exams.

"Have you thought you might be able to use it for finding out about your father? If Stephen agreed." It was the first time for weeks that Chris had spoken of Vicky's search. Even this silence had seemed to Vicky like a sort of reproach. Chris hadn't forgotten, she'd deliberately kept quiet.

She said, "I did think about it. But it probably wouldn't

work, and anyhow I don't want to try. It felt horrible. Stephen didn't like it any more than I did." Saying this brought back the sympathy she and Stephen had shared in their embarrassment, and she felt warmer towards him.

"If you feel like that, why don't you give Steve back that bit of wood? It's really his," Chris said.

"I will some time." Vicky picked it up. She would take it upstairs and hide it away again in her box, until the right moment for handing it over to Stephen. Then, she wasn't sure. Giving it back to Stephen would be a definite gesture of dismissal. Like saying to him, "There you are, there's nothing left to share." She wasn't sure she was ready to do that yet.

"I'm going to wash my bag. Shall I do yours too?" Chris said.

"You mean to get rid of the exam feeling?"

"Something like that."

"Chris!" It would never be the right moment to say what she wanted to, but since Chris herself had introduced the subject, Vicky seized this opportunity.

"Give me your bag, then. Yes? What?"

"You know Dad was saying we should decide where we want to go when he has his holiday?"

"Paul says Weymouth's really nice. Lovely walks, and you can go across to Jersey on a boat."

Vicky said, "I want to go to Cornwall," and saw Chris's face change.

"You mean . . . because of looking for your mother's family?"

"Chris, don't look like that! It isn't as if we hadn't got to think of somewhere new to go to."

"What'd you say to Dad?" Chris asked, running hot water into the washing-up bowl in the sink.

"I wouldn't say why. He wouldn't know."

"I don't see it'd help. Cornwall's big. It isn't as if you could drive about to different places and ask."

"I know all that. Even if I don't find anything, I still want to go."

Silence from Chris.

"If you knew your family had come from somewhere and you'd never been there, wouldn't you want to go? To see what it's like?"

"Suppose I might," Chris said.

"I wouldn't make a fuss about it. I mean, I wouldn't tell Dad. Or do anything so that he'd wonder why."

"How'd we know where to stay? We've only got a month to find a place," Chris said.

"There's adverts in the papers. And places you can go where they tell you about farms and places."

Chris beat up the soapsuds with her hand, then rubbed the two bags vigorously. She'd rinsed them twice in fresh water before she said, "All right."

"Thanks thousands, Chris."

"All the same..."

"I know you don't like it. But I'll be really careful while we're there. And I'll do the finding out about where to go and everything."

"You'd better clear those things off the table before Dad gets back," Chris said. The subject was clearly closed. Vicky took her possessions upstairs and stowed her fragment of the Egg safely away. She didn't want to have to think about the Egg and its effect on her life and on Stephen's. Ordinary living, with exams, Chris's hurt feelings, the possibility of getting to Cornwall, were complications enough for the moment.

A day or two later, Mr. Stanford said, over the evening meal. "Made up your minds where you want to go for the holiday, have you? We haven't got long to book ourselves in."

Vicky said, "What about Falmouth, Dad?"

"Cornwall? Long way," Mr. Stanford said.

"People say it's lovely, though."

"Think we'd get somewhere to stay? Short notice for the seaside."

"There was an advert in the paper the other day. I'll show you..."

The paper was stuck behind the clock. Vicky fetched it and pointed. "There. Says rooms to let and half or full board. I could write off tonight."

"There's a lot of others. What made you pick on that?" Mr. Stanford asked.

"It just sounded nice. I read up about Falmouth in the library. There's boat trips along the coast, and a big harbour and buses that go all over."

Chris's unspoken comment was loud, but Vicky wouldn't take any notice.

"What about you, Chris?" her Dad asked.

"I don't mind," Chris said, untruly.

"All right, then. See what they write back. Don't go booking till you've shown it to me. Two weeks, we'll want, end of July."

"Thanks, Dad."

She sounded too grateful. Mr. Stanford looked at Vicky suspiciously, but all he saw was a head bent over her plate. Chris looked a bit uneasy, but that was natural. He was upset himself. Their first holiday since *she* had gone. It was all the same to him what they did, and if Vicky was set on Falmouth, he'd go along with it. Somewhere new, he wouldn't be reminded all the time.

11

Danny rang Detective Superintendent Price.

"Jim? Danny here. Missing Persons. About that girl."

"What girl?" Snappish. There were dozens of girls in trouble of one kind or another.

"You old sinner! The dark-haired beauty from the west. Cornwall, you said. Remember now?"

"You've found something?" Price asked, surprised. It had been such a shot in the dark.

"Well now, there's more than one ye might think it worth your while to be considering. Will I tell ye about them, or do you want to come over and take your pick? We've some rare beauties here, if you can believe the pictures we have."

"Give me a run down, there's a good fellow. Save me a bit of time, and I need it just now."

"To start with, then, we've a couple of Asian girls from Exeter that didn't like the marriages their families had got arranged for them..."

"Not Asians, Danny. I should have said..."

"You should indeed, Jim Price."

"And another thing. The girl I'm looking for hadn't any family. Yes, I know" – interrupting Danny's vehement exclamation – "I know kids say that when what they mean is they wish it was true. But there's some reason to think this time it was a fact. What does that leave us with?"

There was a snort at the other end of the line.

"How many would that fit?" Price asked again.

"If you'd told me all that at the beginning, I wouldn't be keeping you waiting now." Danny's voice was aggrieved.

"Sorry, Danny. Look! Sort them out, and ring me back if you've found anything, will you?" He was about to ring off, when Danny spoke again.

"I suppose you know, don't you, that half these girls is safely home again now, and no one taking the trouble to be letting anyone know? Quick enough to tell us when the girl goes off, they are, but when she comes back, safe and sound, do they tell us so we can put the record straight? They do not."

"So any one of those girls you've got in the index may not have gone missing for more than a month or so?" It sounded hopeless.

"That's right. Now, while I'm searching for this girl who never had a Dadda and a Mammy, you be considering that." The receiver the other end was slammed down. No wonder Danny was cross.

An hour and a half later, however, he seemed to have recovered his usual good humour.

"You're in luck, Jim Price. There's two left out of all that many. Well, one and a half, really."

"Danny! How can there be half a girl?"

"That's just my manner of speaking. Do you want me to tell you?"

"Please."

"I'll give ye the half first. Just to whet your appetite. Helen Penrose. Age seventeen. Lodged with an aunt in St. Riok..."

"St. what?"

"St. Riok. I'm not a bit wiser than you. That's one saint I never heard on. Will ye listen, now. Lodged in St. Riok, Cornwall. Five foot five, slim build, hair black, skin pale, eyes hazel..."

"Could be Vicky!" thought Price. Aloud he said, "Why doesn't she rate more than a half? Came back home, did she?"

"Not that. But here's the snag. It'll be seventeen years come Christmas that she was reported missing. You said

81

seventeen years or more and that's barely sixteen and a half. That's what I was meaning when I said it's only half the answer."

Price did a quick calculation. Vicky wasn't yet seventeen. He must find out what month she'd been born in. If this girl hadn't gone missing until after Vicky's birth, that ruled her out straight away. He asked, "Was she known to be pregnant at the time?"

A pause. Then, "Nothing to say that on the piece of paper I have here in front of me."

"Got a picture?"

"I have, but it was taken when she was a kid. Ten years old, and it's that blown up from a micro dot, you wouldn't recognize your own mother from it. But here's a curious thing."

"What's that?"

"She lodged with an aunt. No parents, which is what you were asking for . . ."

"What's curious about living with an aunt?" Price asked.

"Isn't it curious that it wasn't the aunt that reported her missing?"

"Who did, then?"

"The village schoolmistress. Mrs. Mary Yelland."

Yelland. Price wrote the name down. He asked, "What was the aunt's name?"

"Hele. H.E.L.E Doris."

"And the girl was Penrose? Is that right?"

"That's right. Good Cornish name."

"What about the other girl? More possible, is she?"

"Ah now. We've got a proper picture. Big girl. Well built. Dark hair, like you said. Might have got to be a regular smasher. She's only young here."

"How young?"

"Fifteen and a half. But by the picture she could have been well over the age of consent."

"And she went missing when?"

"It's eighteen years. So by now she'll be . . . thirty-three. You'd better be minding yourself, Jim Price. These older women is always the worst, you know."

Price said, as good-naturedly as he could, "Shut up, Danny. Stop fooling. Tell me about her."

"Elizabeth Thomas. Came from a home outside Launceston..."

"I said, no family."

"Will ye listen, then? A Home. A Children's Home. Kids in care. Local authority. D'you get the idea? Kids without their Mams and Das. In moral danger. Beaten up. This Elizabeth had been in care since she was three. Never saw her parents, they never visited. When she went missing there was a great search for them, but it seems they'd moved around so no one knew where to look. The brothers and sisters were all in care too, all over the country. Eleven of them. Can you believe it? And they not Catholics either!" Danny sounded as shocked as he'd ever allow himself to be.

"Description?"

"Man, it's always the same. Hair dark, curly, eyes brown. Tall for her age, five foot seven, well built, complexion rosy. Distinguishing mark, scar of old burn on left upper arm. You can stake your soul her loving Mam did that for her with the smoothing iron before the kid went into care. That's the sort of thing they get taken in for. To keep them from being walloped to death by their loving Mams."

"You don't know that!" Price said, more sharply than he meant to.

"Fruits of experience, man, that's all. Anything more I can tell ye?"

"The name of the Home. Launceston, you said?"

"Launceston it is. And the Home was called The Grange."

"Who made the report of this girl's going missing?"

"House mother. Mrs. Jarvis. Mrs. Rose Jarvis."

But eighteen years ago, Price thought. It'd be a rare chance if she was still there. Or that anyone would be able to trace a girl who had disappeared eighteen years ago.

He became aware that Danny was saying something, and listened. "... that all, or is there more you want from me?"

"No. Thanks, Danny, you're a sport. Send over the papers about those two, would you? So I can take a look at the pictures?" He heard Danny's "One and a half lasses coming up, right away," and rang off. Price sat and looked at the silent telephone, thinking over what he'd heard.

The girl from Launceston seemed the likelier bet. She might well have gone off with a boy, got pregnant and had the baby more than a year after leaving the Home. The other one, the Penrose girl, wouldn't fit unless Vicky's birthday was right at the end of the year. But whether Vicky's mother was one of these two, or another unknown girl, it was the same question that bothered Price. What did a young girl, without friends, probably without any training for a job, do, alone in the big city? Living a life so anonymous that no efforts to trace her, either during that life, or after her death, had any success. That meant that she hadn't gone to a doctor, hadn't attended ante-natal clinics, had carried the baby and presumably somehow managed to support herself right up to the moment of birth. She must have walked into a casualty department when the labour began and had the baby. Price imagined that she must have meant to return to that same sort of forlorn existence, but now with the added responsibility of a kid to care for.

She'd have been about the age Vicky was now, or only a year or so older. At the thought of Vicky, the child he knew, wandering around London, homeless, probably hard-up and pregnant, anger took him suddenly and threw him physically off balance. He felt sick. He wondered what had happened to the clumsy, uncaring oaf who had got the girl pregnant and then left her to fend for herself. Probably now he was a prosperous business man or a farmer with a wife and kids, having forgotten all about that earlier affair with a girl who had trusted him too far. Price found himself hoping that the wife was a shrew.

Absurd to get het up. There was no evidence, apart from Mrs. Stanford's testimony that Vicky's mother hadn't been just as irresponsible and uncaring. He wouldn't be surprised to discover that Mrs. Stanford had used her imagination freely on behalf of Vicky's peace of mind.

When the two files were delivered to his office, half an hour later, he looked first at the photographs to see if he could trace any likeness. But Danny had been right. These enlargements from tiny snapshots were as misleading as they were helpful. Both pictures were blurred, smudgy; both girls had dark hair, Elizabeth Thomas's standing out in a cloud round her head, Helen Penrose's longer and flatter. Both had big childish eyes, the Thomas girl's a shade the darker. Helen Penrose looked like a very little girl, Elizabeth Thomas was very nearly a young woman. Disconcerting.

Looking through the papers, however, Price did discover one new fact. Although the report of Helen's disappearance hadn't been made till the December, she had in fact left the village several months earlier. The exact date wasn't clear. Why? But if Vicky's birthday was towards the end of the year, this meant that Helen Penrose was in the running again.

The question was, what should he tell Vicky now?

He decided that it would be cruel and stupid to tell her what he knew to date. He certainly would not volunteer information; if she asked him he would stall. He wouldn't actually say he hadn't done anything. He could use one of the common police evasions – "enquiries are being made" ... "progress is reported along certain lines." Jargon. Usually he had no use for it. But he would at least let her know that he hadn't put the whole thing right out of his mind. He'd emphasize the difficulty in following a trail more than seventeen years cold. If he ever found himself in that part of the country he might go and see if anyone at The Grange remembered Mrs. Jarvis or Elizabeth Thomas. If that proved a red herring, the village with the outlandish saint's name wasn't too far away, he might look up the village schoolmistress there; though Danny was right, there wasn't more than half a chance of the Penrose girl being the right one.

Price sighed. He had more pressing affairs to look into

which needed his full concentration. He turned back to the study of the case of the bullion van, waylaid by a couple of thugs disguised as patrolling police officers. Silver worth half a million had been taken and was now stashed away somewhere. He'd have to work fast to stop it being smuggled out of the country.

12

Falmouth was hot and crowded and steep. The rooms they'd taken were high up, in the residential part of the town, and though it was true that you could see the sea from the upper windows, it took a good twenty minutes to get there and, because of the hill, much longer to get back. But there were good things about the place too. You could go to the further side of Pendennis Point and find beaches to swim from, or rocks, if you felt brave and wanted fewer people around.

"Ugh-gh! Cold!" Chris gasped the first time she went in.

"Can't be colder than Lowestoft," Vicky, still struggling into her bathing cap, said.

"'Tis. Icy."

"I suppose it's because of there being so much more of the Atlantic," Vicky said through chattering lips, when she was also in the water.

"What about the Gulf Stream, then?"

They had to laugh. Mrs. Greenston, the young and pretty teacher who took them for geography, had had a thing about the Gulf Stream. All her lessons about the British Isles seemed sooner or later to require an explanation of the Gulf Stream and the difference it had made to British geology, flora and fauna, and also to British history.

"Gulf Stream! You could have fooled me," Vicky said, climbing out on to rocks worn smooth by aeons of pounding Atlantic waves, and shaking sea water from her goose-pimpled arms and legs.

"Dad's right. Swimming in that isn't much fun," Chris said, towelling vigorously.

"I dunno. It feels terrific. Like . . . soda water."

"It's just the same water as the other side. The North Sea."

"It doesn't feel the same. Bouncier."

"That's just waves."

"Looks different too. It's clear here. Look! Where it's calm, between the rocks, you can see right down to the bottom. Not muddy like at Lowestoft."

"You like it because it's Cornish," Chris said.

"Not because it's Cornish. Because it's beautiful."

"I meant, because you know about your mother. Like you say you like those yellow buns . . ."

"Saffron."

". . . and those awful pasties we had for supper last night."

"I didn't like them. I only said you could make pasties taste good if they weren't just old potatoes and a stock cube."

But Vicky saw that she'd been careless. She didn't want to hurt Chris's feelings more than she must. She owed Chris a lot for not letting on to their Dad the real reason for her sudden interest in coming to Falmouth. It was up to her now to keep quiet, to pretend that this was just an ordinary holiday, and that all she wanted was to go on the little pleasure boats or the buses and to see as much of the county as they could.

"Do you think Dad's enjoying it?" she asked Chris as they climbed the hill back towards their lodgings.

"Not enjoying it, exactly. But I think he's all right."

"He really liked it when we took the boat to the Helford River, didn't he?"

"I think so. It's difficult to be sure, with Dad."

"I wonder if he's ever been the sort of person who talks about what he's feeling," Vicky said.

"Shouldn't think so. He didn't have to with Mum. She'd have been the one to tell him what he was feeling. As well as what she was."

88

"She didn't do it to us, though, did she? Not like Stephen says his father does. You know. Explaining everything all the time."

"Mum didn't need to explain. She knew, and she knew we knew."

Vicky said, "It's funny. I thought going somewhere new would mean I wouldn't think about her so much, only..."

"I know. I'm like that too. I keep on thinking, 'I must bring Mum here to see this'..." Chris said.

"That's it! She'd have loved those birds we saw out at the Helford."

"Or that old pub we went to on the coach..."

She'd have understood what I'm feeling now, too, Vicky thought. She might not have said, but she'd have known I have to think about my own Mum while I'm here. Every new place we see, I'm wondering if this was where she lived before she came up to London. But now that she was here, in Cornwall, Vicky had begun to realize what a hopeless quest she was on. It had been idiotic to suppose that here, in this tangle of rocks and scrub and moorland and tiny villages, she could discover any more than she might have been able to in London.

And in London, there was Detective Chief Superintendent Price, who would help if he could.

From a long way away, she heard Chris's voice.

"What'll you and Dad do?"

"What? When? What d'you mean, what'll we do?"

"You weren't listening. I said, when Paul comes down this weekend, he'll want for us to go off for a bit on our own. What'll you and Dad do?"

"We could go on another of those boat trips. Or just go down to the harbour. Dad likes that."

"You don't mind?" Chris asked.

"Course not. It's nice that Mike could give Paul a lift. He'll love it here."

"I'd like him to see it," Chris said, and Vicky thought that it would be nice, too, for Paul to see Chris, sunburned to a delicious Cox's Orange apple browny-pink, with streaks of pale gold in her hair. She wished she burned pinky-brown and gold, instead of sallow. She wished she had Chris's calm acceptance of what happened. She wondered... "If it had been Chris who'd been the adopted one, would she worry?"

Paul duly arrived on the back of Mike's motor bike. He and Chris went off that Saturday afternoon, and Vicky and Mr. Stanford wandered down through the steep streets of the town, huddled on the edge of the harbour. Little alleys gave them sudden glimpses of bright blue water and sunlight. They walked along the dockside, empty on this Saturday afternoon of workers.

"Dead ground," Mr. Stanford said.

"Why dead, Dad?"

"Work's all gone. Abroad. Used to be one of the great shipyards in the country. Look at it now."

There were, indeed, only two or three ships to be seen in dock.

"Why? Why aren't there more ships in here?" Vicky asked.

"Too expensive. Work isn't done on time, so the orders don't come in."

"But whose fault is that? Isn't it partly because of strikes?" Vicky ventured.

"Why do you think they strike? It isn't for fun. Money's not good enough."

Vicky sat, warmed by the sun, contemplating the decay of Britain's great past. She didn't know enough to pursue the subject. Her Dad sat beside her, apparently engrossed in his own thoughts. He surprised her by saying, suddenly, "Chris and Paul. They're serious?"

It was so unlike him to embark on talk about their personal lives, that for a moment Vicky couldn't collect her thoughts. Eventually she said, "Chris thinks they are."

"What has she told you?"

"Told me she thought they'd get married. Not now. One day."

Silence.

"He's a clever lad," Mr. Stanford said at last.

"Chris has liked him for ages."

90

"He'd look after her all right."

"Yes."

Another long silence. Vicky wondered if they should be moving on.

"After they're married. I don't want. You feeling you've to stay. On. Just to see to me," Mr. Stanford said, in a series of staccato utterances.

Vicky was too much surprised to say anything.

"You've your own life to lead. I don't want to be a burden. If you want to go to college. That's what you do."

"I don't know," Vicky said.

"You're clever."

"I don't know if I'm clever enough."

"Mum thought you'd go to college. She didn't think Chris would. She always said you were different."

"If I did go . . . If it meant going away . . ."

"Well? What?"

"If Chris was married. You'd be all by yourself."

"You haven't to think about that. Kids shouldn't be sacrificed for their parents. It's not right," Mr. Stanford said.

There was too much they couldn't say to each other. Vicky wanted to ask, "If I'd been your real daughter? Would you feel like that about me then?" As if he'd heard the thought, her Dad said, "I'd say the same if it was you going steady and Chris that wanted to go away for some sort of training."

"I'm not going to get married."

"Wait till you're asked," Mr. Stanford said, almost as his wife might have.

"Dad?"

"What?"

"Did Mum look like Chris? When you first met her?"

"She wasn't pretty like Chris. But there was something about her."

He paused.

"Go on, Dad."

"I was like you. I didn't mean to marry."

"Mum changed your mind?" Vicky asked.

"I suppose that's what happened. I used to tell her . . ."

91

"What?"

"Said she made up her mind to marry me and I hadn't a chance." He got up abruptly. "Come on. We'll take the boat across to St. Mawes and have one of your Cornish teas. Chris and Paul won't be back in a hurry."

It was the most intimate conversation they had ever had. As they sat on the small packed steamer that made the short journey across the harbour to St. Mawes, Vicky tried to look at Dad as if he were a new person, as if she'd never seen him before. A middling-sized, middle-aged man, with thick grey hair, a jutting nose, very bright eyes under heavy grey eyebrows. He looked determined, forceful: a man who would always think for himself. He'd been the stern one when they were little, she and Chris. Almost all the discipline had come from him. And something more. Vicky remembered an occasion years and years ago, when she and Chris had been really small. They had quarrelled over something ... yes, a doll's cradle. Vicky had been playing with it and Chris had taken it for her koala bear. In the ensuing squabble, Mum had slapped them both and told them to play with something else. It had been Dad who had asked for the facts of the case, and had established Vicky's right, since she'd taken the cradle out of the toybox first, to keep it for as long as she wanted on that occasion. Vicky could recall now the relief when what had seemed like injustice had been righted. Mum had been impartially loving, but Dad had wanted justice for each of them.

She couldn't tell him. Chris would have. Mum would have. All Vicky could manage was an extra pang of guilt that she'd brought Dad all this way down to Cornwall in the hope of finding another father. That was not giving him back the justice he deserved from her.

13

It had been hot in London that week, and Price was restless. The bullion snatch no longer held any interest for him; five of the men involved were now in custody, and the sixth should be arriving back in the country any day now, under an extradition order. Some of the bullion had reappeared, the rest had probably gone for ever. There were other cases, of course, still open-ended; some of them had been dragging on for months. But nothing urgent. Price sat in his office and looked out over the great city, spread out below him like an aerial photograph, and wished he were almost anywhere else.

He said this to Jill Peabody as she put a sheaf of paper on his desk.

"Why don't you take a few days off?" she asked.

"Wouldn't do any good. Don't take any notice of me, Jill. I'm always like this in the summer. I'll be all right when the weather cools down. Or when the next case comes along."

"It'd do you good to get out into the country," Jill Peabody said.

"What'd I do in the country?"

"Walk? Or you could go somewhere where there's fishing. Or the sea. You could swim."

"What do you do on holiday?" Price asked.

"My Mum and Dad live in Sussex. I go there, mostly."

"Brought up in the country, were you?" Price asked, and thought how odd it was that he knew practically nothing about this young woman whom he'd now been seeing almost every day for over a year.

"Birmingham. Couldn't you tell by the accent?" she said. The words gave him an uncomfortable jolt. For a moment he couldn't think why. Then he remembered Vicky, and her voice on the telephone. How long ago? Two months. Three. He hadn't heard from her again. He hadn't done anything either, about the two girls Danny had unearthed, missing from Launceston and the unknown village in Cornwall. He didn't at the moment remember their names. But he felt bad. He shouldn't ever have told Vicky he'd try to help. He wasn't often soft like that. But there was something about Vicky that touched him. He'd have liked to be able to do something for her. Not necessarily find her lost family. That didn't always turn out the most wonderful success in his experience. She had probably done as well as possible for herself by having that nice woman who'd adopted her for a mother, and Chris for a sister. In any case, she was growing up now, and it wouldn't be long before she found the right boy and started a family of her own.

He couldn't dismiss the thought aroused by Jill's remarks. Later in the morning he looked through the papers he'd been dealing with last April. At first he couldn't find what he wanted, then, on a space in his diary at the appropriate date, he found the scribbled names he'd been searching for. Helen Penrose. St. Riok. Mrs. Mary Yelland. Mrs. Hele. Mrs. Jarvis. The Grange. Elizabeth Thomas.

"Ever been to Cornwall?" he asked Jill.

"Once, when I was a kid. Lovely big beaches. Waves were a bit scary, though. Why? Thinking of going there?"

He'd thought he was going to give an emphatic "No." Instead, to his own surprise, he heard his voice say, "Might think about it. Some time."

He hadn't been as casual as he'd have liked. Jill looked at him quickly. She said, "Something special? Or just a break?"

"Someone I might look up."

"Give you something to do that isn't fishing or swim-

94

ming," she said, smiling at him.

How terrible, Price thought, as he tidied his desk before leaving, if he'd become one of those people who are incapable of taking real time off work. Coming out into the aching heat of Victoria Street, he longed suddenly for a respite from grinding gears and the smell of car exhausts. He thought, "I could go and have a look at the places. See the women, Mrs. Jarvis, Mrs. Yelland, if they're still there. Then, if there's anything to know, I could tell Vicky. Let her down gently." He found that he hated the thought that Vicky might come across some devastating piece of news which she wouldn't be able to cope with. He didn't know exactly what sort of news it might be, he simply wanted to protect her from disappointment, or, worse, from disillusion.

"I'm middle-aged. I'm an idiot," he thought. He, if anyone, should know that there is no sure protection against disappointment and disillusion. Not just in his professional life. After his experience with Laurie, he'd thought he'd never look at another woman. Perhaps the solitary, reserved life he'd led since then, for the last fifteen years, had been cowardly, a half-conscious fear of getting as much hurt as that again. Stupid! There is no stronghold you can build, no armour you can forge for yourself, or for anyone else, which is a certain insurance against pain, without as well the shutting out of life. Was that the mistake he'd made with Laurie? Tried to keep her safe from all possible harm, and in the process cut her off from some of the living she needed, was entitled to? Perhaps he hadn't trusted enough then to the strengths that Laurie could have found in herself or, later, to his own power of recovery. His colleagues would have found it unbelievable that Jim Price had ever lived in an ivory tower, but as far as his own personal life went, he began to wonder if this wasn't the truth.

There was a travel agency, open late, in the street he was crossing. On impulse, he went in and asked for information about St. Riok. A fatigued girl, sweating in the heat of this stifling July day, looked up the name for him in a railway guide. It wasn't there. Then in a file of holiday resorts. She told him, finally, doubtfully, that it was really tiny, just a few shops and houses on the edge of a newish holiday camp site. Inland, about a mile or two from the coast. There were some well-known beaches near. Whitesands? Had he heard of that? Trelore? The Mare Sands?

He'd never heard of any of them. He doubted if the girl had either.

"Nearest town is Lodenek," she offered him.

"Where's that?"

She showed him on the map. It was at the mouth of an estuary. She read him bits out of the brochure. There was a golf course. Sailing. Mackerel fishing. No rail link. You could take the train to Bodmin Road . . . He said that if he went he'd be driving anyway.

He spent the week-end mulling it over. On the Monday morning he packed an overnight bag and rang Jill Peabody to tell her he was taking her advice and going away for three or four nights. Gave her the names of Launceston, Lodenek. If anything really urgent came up, she could get in touch with the local Stations. He'd drop in to see if there were any messages. This reminded him to get in touch with the Chief Constable of the Districts he'd be visiting. A courtesy gesture which didn't tie him down to doing more than looking in on the constabulary to see if he was needed back here. He didn't mean, anyhow, to be away for more than the coming week. He got out his little Fiat and started off along the M4 for the West. He told himself he must be crazy.

He didn't drive fast. That had never been his way. But on a clear road, and influenced by the cars which shot past him, he found he was doing sixty without knowing it. By the late afternoon he was the further side of Exeter, on a road that twisted up and down the lush Devonshire valleys, then on a stretch of high ground. He went through Moretonhampstead, making his way towards Launceston. Crossed the River Tamar, which for so long kept Cornwall practically unknown territory, but was here a small stream, spanned by an unimpressive small stone bridge. Came to the hill leading up to the gaunt walls of Launceston itself, drove in, parked the car by the side of a park and went on foot in search of information.

He hesitated between the Town Hall and the police station, but decided, partly because he came on it first, that the station would be more likely to provide what he wanted quickly. He introduced himself and asked about a Children's Home in the neighbourhood. The Grange. An elderly officer knew about it, but the message was disappointing. The Home had been given up nine years previously, when it had been badly damaged by fire. Probably started by one of the young devils they had living there. Since then it had been completely re-built and was now a luxury hotel.

"And Mrs. Jarvis?"

The officer didn't know the name. The last matron had been a Mrs. Willis. She had been there for a couple of years before the fire. Which meant, Price saw, that she wouldn't have been there with the missing Elizabeth Thomas.

He had another thought. "Did the children in the Home go to the local schools?"

The officer thought they had. Different schools in Launceston and in the village.

Where would the records of the Home be now?

With the Social Department at the Town Hall. But there wouldn't be anyone there this late. Tomorrow . . .

Tomorrow he might look them up. Try to discover which school Elizabeth Thomas had attended. Then look for people in their thirties who'd been pupils with her. It was a daunting task.

He decided that he didn't like Launceston, didn't want to stay the night. He'd go off towards Lodenek and pursue the other girl. At least he'd be asking questions in a small village, and if the village schoolmistress, this Mrs. Mary Yelland, was still alive, she'd be able to tell him enough to show whether it was worth his while to come back here. He drove in the failing light across Bodmin Moor, astonished at the emptiness and wildness of the great expanse of heaving country. Too dark now to see what it was really like. He might have a look at it in daylight. He reached

97

Bodmin, a grey granite town with narrow streets, no more inviting than Launceston. But he'd gone far enough for one day. He found a place that called itself a hotel, but was really no more than a pub with a room or two above. Lucky to get that, he supposed, right in the middle of the holiday season. He had a poor meal, quickly unfrozen, he guessed, for all that the menu was self-consciously Cornish, and went up to a small, impersonal room. The bed was lumpy, but the night air, when he'd persuaded the sticky sash window to open, was sweet. Tomorrow he'd pursue this wild-goose-chase a step further. He went to sleep calling himself every kind of a fool.

14

It was in St. Mawes that Vicky saw it.

St. Mawes was a village made for tourists. Every shop sold souvenirs: lucky pixies, wooden plaques inscribed with Cornish proverbs or prayers in pokerwork, models of ships, the usual gumph. Every cottage had a notice that here Cornish teas were served; there were yachts tied up in the water all round, and the narrow street was thronged with people on holiday.

Vicky and her dad had had their tea – "didn't think the cream was up to much", Mr. Stanford had said – and they were wandering back towards the pier, where the small steamer was waiting for them, when Vicky's eye was caught by something in one of the tourist-trap shop windows. She stopped, went back a step or two and looked again. Mr. Stanford, separated from her by the crowd, went on without noticing that she was not directly behind him.

Vicky looked and looked again. She couldn't believe it. She saw her Dad, well ahead of her, twenty yards along the road. She went into the shop.

It was full of people fingering things. "Just looking", as they would have said. There were two customers at the small counter buying stickers for their cars, teaspoons with coats of arms on the handles and other interesting and necessary objects. There were only two women serving. Vicky had to wait.

The purchaser in front of her was taking for ever to

decide between two pokerwork mottoes. The other was one of those shoppers who seem to have finished and then add on first one, then another, then a third item. The woman serving her was already bored with ringing up the total, giving the change, and then being asked to start again. To the embroidered tray cloth the buyer added a mug; then she decided she must have two mugs. Then she thought an ashtray would be useful. Just as Vicky thought she really had finished, her husband, pushing his way through the crowded shop, said, "Got something for Sally?" She hadn't, and the whole business seemed about to start again.

The steamer hooted. Dad would be worried. And angry. Vicky said desperately, "Can I just ask something?"

The woman buyer turned a good-tempered irresolute face toward her. The woman on the other side of the counter, her patience exhausted, said, "I'm serving. Can't you see?"

"I'm sorry . . . but I've got to rush . . . I'm going back to Falmouth . . . Please!"

"Go on, you ask away," the irresolute one said.

"It's that shawl. In the window . . ."

"Twenty-eight pounds," the seller said.

"Hand-knitted, I suppose?" the irresolute woman asked.

"That's right. Very unique. You won't find anything like that anywhere else . . ."

"Where? I mean, who makes them?" Vicky managed to insert into what seemed no longer to be her conversation.

"Old lady. Not from round here. It's a bargain, there won't be many more. She must be eighty if she's a day," the selling woman said, not to Vicky but to the other woman, who seemed a more likely customer.

"Really? But twenty-eight! That's a lot of money, even for nowadays . . ."

"But where? Where does she live?" Vicky asked. The steamer hooted again.

"I said, not from round here."

"Where from?"

"Little place the other side. St. Riok. Quite a way off.

100

There isn't anyone in these parts who knows the pattern. My daughter, she lives over there, see? It's her picks them up for me when the old lady's finished one, and that's not more than once in six months..."

Vicky fled.

She was the last passenger to hurl herself down the gangway and Mr. Stanford was cross.

"What happened to you? Why didn't you come on the boat when I did?"

"I stopped to look at something in a shop, and there were such a lot of people."

"Rubbish those shops have. I don't know why you want to waste your money..."

"I didn't buy anything.

"Then what took so long? If you'd missed this boat you might have had to stay for another two hours."

"I'm sorry. I couldn't get at you to tell you..."

"Nothing in those places you can't get anywhere ... I've always told you, you should keep together in a crowd."

It was an unfortunate end to their excursion. Vicky said she was sorry again and Mr. Stanford grunted his acceptance of the apology, but the feeling of confidence between them had gone. They hardly spoke on the way back.

At the early supper, Chris and Paul kept the conversation going, and there was no need for her to do more than appear to listen. Afterwards Chris and Paul went off to look at the sea as it got dark, but Vicky, saying she was tired, which wasn't true, stayed in the stuffy little sitting room, pretending to read. Presently her Dad went off for a pint and a game of darts at the local, and she was left alone to think.

The shawl. The shawl in the shop window. She couldn't have been mistaken. It had the same lacy pattern as the shawl wrapped in white paper in her Mum's bottom drawer. Different from other lacy knitting because of the alternation of the motifs and the edging, which had a scalloped look. She'd asked Mum once how you did that sort of knitting, and Mrs. Stanford had said cheerfully, "Don't ask me, love. I couldn't do it any more than fly."

But there was an old lady. Eighty years old. Living at St. Riok wherever that was, still knitting these shawls. She might know something.

Vicky went to the door of Mrs. Rodd's sitting room, which was also the kitchen, and knocked on the door. Mrs. Rodd put out a head covered with Saturday evening curlers and said, "You wanting something?"

"Just I wanted to ask . . . Where's St. Riok?"

Mrs. Rodd looked mystified. "Is it one of the churches, dear?"

"I think it's a place," Vicky said.

"Somewhere near here, is it?"

"No, I think it's quite far away."

"Sorry, dear, can't help you. There's plenty of names like that round here. Saints I've never heard of. It wasn't St. Just, you wanted?"

"No. St. Riok."

"Not St. Austell?"

"St. Riok," Vicky said.

"Might be anywhere," Mrs. Rodd said helpfully.

"Have you got a map? That I could borrow?"

"No, sorry, dear. I can't seem to get on with maps. Places all seem to look different on a map."

Vicky had to give it up. And the next day would be Sunday, all the shops shut, no hope of finding a map anywhere. It was maddening.

She was too cross and too het up to sleep. But by the time Chris came to bed she had had an idea.

"Chris! Do you think Mike . . ."

"Did I wake you? I was trying to be ever so quiet."

"I haven't been asleep. Do you think . . ."

"Paul thinks it's beautiful too," Chris said in a warm, contented voice.

"Oh! Sorry, I meant to ask. Did you have a good time?"

"Lovely. We walked right out on the cliffs, miles. Well, a long way."

"Chris, I wanted to ask. . . ?"

"What?" Chris said, stepping out of her clothes neatly and standing near-naked in the small bedroom.

102

"D'you think Mike's got a map? Of Cornwall?"

"I expect he has. He must have, mustn't he? Why?"

Caution made Vicky say, "Just something someone said. I wondered if we'd go somewhere different next week."

"I'll ask Paul tomorrow." The bedsprings creaked.

"How long's he staying?"

"They've got to start back about six. Evening."

"Will Paul be seeing Mike before that? After he's come round here in the morning?"

"Shouldn't think so. Anyway, what's the hurry?"

Vicky didn't answer. She lay awake for what seemed like hours, listening to the sound of Chris's light, even breathing.

15

Vicky had to try to appear neither anxious nor impatient for the whole of the next day; and when Mike did eventually turn up to take Paul back to London, he was so much behind time that it wasn't possible to ask if she could look at his maps, without making too much fuss. She had to wait till Monday morning, when she suggested that they should go to the coach station to discover what other places there were to see in their last week.

"I like just walking around and looking at things here," Chris said.

"But there's lots of things we ought to see."

"Like what?"

"Tintagel, where King Arthur lived. Well, I don't suppose he did really, but he's supposed to have. Or Land's End. Or St. Michael's Mount. There's all sorts of places we haven't been to."

"Can't say I fancy being stuck in a coach all day," Mr. Stanford said.

"Anyway, you don't mind if I go and have a look?"

She went off alone, which was what she'd hoped for. She didn't go to the coach station, but to the tourist office, where a brisk young man looked up St. Riok for her in a large file.

"Just a little village. On the coast road to Northsea. Nothing there, as far as I can see."

"Nothing at all? But it is a village?"

"Very small. I suppose there's a church, though it isn't

104

mentioned, so it won't be worth going to look at. Near an old airfield that's been made into a sort of holiday camp."

It sounded terrible. Vicky asked, "Isn't it near somewhere interesting?"

"Near Lodenek. That's a nice old town. A lot of visitors go there, especially when they have their festival. But that was back in May."

"Are there coach tours to Lodenek from here?"

The young man said there were, but he was not enthusiastic. He offered Vicky St. Ives, where there was an artists' colony – he made it sound like a collection of rare birds, Vicky thought, all sitting on the sea front waiting for visitors to come and take pictures of them. Or the Lizard – "very spectacular" – or, of course, Tintagel and Boscastle – "very romantic". But Vicky was firm that she wasn't interested in anything but Lodenek. She came away with a leaflet about the coaches in her hand.

"I thought you wanted to see Tintagel," Chris said when shown the leaflet.

"I'd rather see Lodenek. It's where people used to emigrate to America from."

"I don't think that sounds very exciting."

"And they build boats there."

"I suppose Dad might be interested. Would you, Dad?"

"It says here there are numerous walks all round the estuary and along the magnificent coastline."

"All right. I don't mind," Chris said, giving in too suddenly for Vicky's peace of mind. Sure enough, when they were alone that afternoon, Chris said, "You've found out something about your mother."

"How did you know?"

"The way you went on about Lodenek. What is it?"

"It was Saturday. When Dad and I went across to St. Mawes. There was this knitted shawl in a shop and the woman said it came from a village . . ."

"A *shawl*?"

"Don't you remember the one Mum had up in her chest of drawers? That my mother had knitted? With that pattern Mum said she'd never seen anywhere else?"

105

"Like cobwebs? And there're shells in it. Mum always said it could have been made by spiders. What's that got to do with Lodenek?"

"The shop woman said the old lady who'd knitted it lives near Lodenek. In a village. St. Riok."

"How'll you find her if she's just somewhere near?"

"I got the man in the tourist place to show me on a map. It doesn't look too far. I could walk there once we're in Lodenek," Vicky said.

Chris looked at Vicky's face and said, "I suppose you must."

"Really I must."

"I'd better get Dad to go for one of the walks, then, hadn't I? To see the magnificent coastline. Or something."

"*Would* you? Chris . . . I'm sorry . . ."

"All right. I just don't want Dad to know . . ."

Chris hadn't meant to hurt, but this protection of their Dad against what she was going to do, made Vicky feel pushed out, separated by a barrier. If that barrier had been put up by her own actions, it didn't make the feeling any easier to bear.

The next day they were all three in the coach roaring its way across Cornwall. White dusty roads full of holiday traffic, narrow, narrow streets between grey granite housefronts. Steep hills, lushly tree-ed river valleys. Truro, a green copper spire stuck on the side of the cathedral. Open country broken by dry stone walls and hedges into tiny fields. Caravan sites, in the distance the sugar-loaf white mounds of china clay workings. It was a bumpy journey and boring, until suddenly they were grinding down one of the steepest hills yet, into a huddle of houses clinging to the sides of the incline. The coach drew up in front of a small hotel by the side of a little harbour, where fishing boats squatted on the mud of a low tide. This was Lodenek. On the further side of a wide expanse of sand and water was another shore.

"Over there's Trebison. Ferry goes across about every quarter of an hour," the driver said, leaning down from his

106

high seat behind the wheel to instruct his passengers as they got out.

"It just looks like all sand," Chris said, screwing up her eyes against the dazzle of the sun on water.

"Golf course. There's sailing, too, bit further up, when the tide's in. Or there's Trebison church. Used to be right under the sand. They'd let the parson down by rope once a year to say the service. That's what they tell."

"What shall we do, Dad?" Chris asked.

"Let's have a look round this place first, now we're here. We'd better get something to eat, too, before we go across, if that's what you want."

They wandered round the small town. It didn't take long. Two streets of shops, the everyday sort selling food, tools, clothes, alternating with the shops for tourists, all gifts and clutter. Vicky looked in the windows as closely as she could without causing any comments, but there was not a single shawl.

On the pavement outside a café overlooking the harbour, they sat and ate hamburgers and drank Pepsi Cola. The tide was rising, and the boats lifted gently off the bottom. Before the meal was finished, they were rocking in shallow water. Beyond the far jetty, the sand was disappearing fast, and a sheet of shining water separated the two sides of the estuary. The ferry boat came swishing in, unloaded its passengers at the jetty steps, then chugged out with a fresh lading.

"Let's go across and see the buried church," Chris said.

"I don't mind," Mr. Stanford said.

Chris looked at Vicky.

"Do you mind if I don't come too?"

"What'll you do here? You've seen everything, haven't you?" Mr. Stanford said.

"I might walk along by the river towards the sea."

"This is the sea, isn't it?"

"It doesn't look like proper sea. Not when you can see the other side. I like it when you can't see anything, only sky," Vicky said.

"Suit yourself. What about you, Chris? Would you rather

go for a walk with Vicky? I can sit here in the sun. See if that fellow with the rod catches anything."

"No, I want to go in the ferry," Chris said.

Mr. Stanford heaved himself up.

"We'd best go and join the queue over there, then. What time did that driver say the coach started back?"

"Half-five," Chris said.

"If we don't see you before that, we'll see you then. And mind! Don't you be late, like you were at St. Mawes," Mr. Stanford said to Vicky.

"I won't. I'll be there in plenty of time."

Mr. Stanford and Chris went off to the far pier. Vicky found a point from which she could see them embark. She wanted to be sure they were safely on their way before she started her own journey.

She took the Northsea road out of Lodenek. That meant walking up the hill the coach had rumbled down. It was a long hill and even steeper than she'd realized. The signpost told her that St. Riok was two and a half miles off, but long before she got there, she felt as if it was more like three or four. There were more hills, just as steep. She passed farms, fields of sheep, isolated bungalows and cottages. Cars full of children passed her continuously. It was the beginning of the afternoon, families were setting out for picnics on the sand. She tried not to think about families. But it wasn't easy. There were mothers and fathers dragging reluctant children, or with toddlers in pushchairs, walking, like her, along the hot white road, but, unlike her, taking the side roads which led to beaches: Trelore, Whitesands. Some of the cars that passed her were nearly empty, they held only the driver or one passenger. If she'd been one of those drivers, she thought, she'd have offered a lift to a solitary girl walking up and down those hills.

She was not only tired, she was anxious. Suppose when she reached St. Riok, no one knew anything about an old lady who knitted shawls with this fancy pattern? How could she describe the pattern to someone who'd never seen it? She ought to have got the woman in St. Mawes to give her the old lady's name. But it had been such a hurried

108

and interrupted conversation, it hadn't occurred to her at the time. This thought produced fresh anxiety. It was already nearly an hour since she'd left Lodenek. If she was to spend any time at all in the village, she'd hardly have time to walk back. If she was late again, when the coach was due to start back, Dad would be angry, and with reason. She'd have to ignore one of Mum's strictest rules, and try to hitch a lift.

The houses that had been dotted occasionally along the road began to be clustered closer together. She passed a tiny, unofficial-looking police station. Then there was a sign by the side of the road. St. Riok. She had arrived.

She walked on to a crossroads. Here there were shops. A butcher, a greengrocer, a post office which was also a stationer and tobacconist. She chose the biggest shop, which appeared to sell everything from tin buckets and spades to frozen chicken and hair slides. Someone here was sure to know the people who lived around.

Inside the store, Vicky found a girl of about her own age, tidying shelves of chocolates and sweets. She started saying "I wanted to ask..." and then stopped, unsure what exactly she was going to say.

The girl smiled at her. She said, "Can I help you?" in the slowed-down, burred West Country tones which Vicky had been hearing for the last week and which might, she imagined, echo her mother's voice. It gave her courage to say, "I'm looking for a lady who knits. Shawls. I saw one in a shop..."

"That's Mrs. Godfrey. But ... I don't think..."

"She's died?" Vicky could hear the clipped voice of the saleswoman in St. Mawes, as she'd said, "There won't be many more, she must be eighty if she's a day..."

"Mrs. Godfrey's all right. It's her eyes. She can't see to do those fancy stitches any more, that's all."

Vicky's heart hammered. "Does she live round here? Could I see her, d'you suppose?"

The girl considered Vicky. Then she said, "She won't tell you the pattern. She won't tell anyone. There's been plenty of people come asking, but she's always told them, No."

"I don't want the pattern. I just want to ask her something . . . She must have told it to someone. Some time."

"May have. When she was younger. Not now," the girl said.

"Where does she live?" Vicky asked.

The girl looked towards the shop door and pointed. "You can see her cottage from here. That one, with the blue flowers outside the gate."

Vicky said, "Thanks," gratefully. Then, turning back, she said, "Is there anyone in the village called Morgan?"

The girl shook her head. "Don't know anyone."

"Or living somewhere near?"

"Might be in Lodenek. I wouldn't know."

Vicky walked out into the hot white sunlight, towards the cottage. It wasn't a cottage, really. It was a bungalow, separated from the road by a stone wall topped by shrubs. The blue flower was a hydrangea, spreading exuberantly over the entrance.

As she rang the pushbutton bell, Vicky wished she'd never come. One thing to imagine this journey of discovery, another to find yourself in the middle of it. Standing on unknown doorsteps, preparing questions to ask of total strangers, having to be ready to say why you were there, what it meant to you. But she couldn't go back now. Having got so far, she'd got to go on.

The sudden opening of the door took her by surprise. She hadn't heard the sound of approaching footsteps, and when she saw the slippered feet of the tiny old lady she understood why.

"Is it the electricity?" the old lady said at once.

"No. I came to ask . . ."

"If it's the lifeboats, I gave her twenty p last week."

"No. It's . . ."

"I haven't got any more jumble. They took the lot," the old lady said, starting to shut the door.

"Please . . ."

"What is it then? Quick, mind. I'm watching my serial on the telly, and I don't like missing it," the old lady said.

"Mrs. Godfrey?" Vicky asked, though the lady's age and

110

the knitting needles she was clutching in the hand that wasn't on the door, seemed identification enough.

"That's right. I'm Mrs. Godfrey. You'd better come in, then. But you mustn't be long," the old lady said. She shut the door behind Vicky and went surprisingly quickly along the passage towards the open door of a room from which came the sounds of a mid-afternoon television series. Vicky followed.

The small sitting room was crowded, and all the furniture seemed to be congregated round a large television, like worshippers round a sacred relic. The old lady sat herself down on one of the easy chairs and fixed her eyes on the television screen. From her knitting needles depended a long olive-green scarf in plain garter stitch. No more fancy knitting.

"Please!" Vicky said again. She had to speak loudly to be heard above the American voices coming at high volume from the box.

"Go on, then. What's it all about?" the old lady said, not taking her eyes from the screen.

"I saw a shawl you'd knitted. At St. Mawes . . ."

"In the shop?" the old lady asked.

"That's right. And the woman said . . ."

"What was she asking for it?" the old lady said sharply.

"Twenty-eight pounds. But . . ."

"I wouldn't let her have another if there was twenty more. Ten. That's all she gave me. Barely pays for the wool. I told her . . ."

"It's the pattern," Vicky began.

"Hush a minute. I want to hear what this one says." The old lady leaned forward. Her needles continued to clack while she listened to some supremely funny conversation between two of the characters on the screen. Vicky wasn't listening. She heard a jumble of sounds that didn't make any sense. The old lady rocked with mirth.

"Best of the lot, he is. The others, sometimes they aren't hardly comic at all, but that one, he always makes me laugh."

"That one" had now left the screen. Vicky tried again.

"The lady in the shop said you were the only person who knew that pattern. The shawl," she said.

"That's right. And I'm not telling it, if that's what you've come for."

"Didn't anyone else ever know it? Didn't you tell anyone?" Vicky asked. The importance of the question made her tremble.

"One or two I may have told. Not the young ones. They never wanted to know. Too much trouble. Here she comes! Oooh, look at that! Did you ever? At this time of day!"

Vicky did look at the picture on the screen. A well-built young woman, wearing very few clothes, was tripping into a sitting room where two other women and several men were looking at her with different expressions of dislike, envy and lust.

"She's always bold, but I never seen anything like that!" the tiny old lady said, knitting faster than ever.

"Who did you tell? Can't you remember their names?" Vicky asked.

"Their names? I don't bother with their names. Except she's Mavis. I do know that," the old lady said, impatient.

"Not the telly. The pattern. The people you told about the pattern?"

"*Them*? Oh, them. No, I don't. I might've told Mary. I don't remember. Oh, she's saucy! Isn't she saucy? Wouldn't you say she's as saucy as they come?" the old lady maddeningly replied.

"Please! Couldn't you try to remember? Just for a minute? Who did you tell about the shawl pattern?" Vicky implored. But this time the old lady did not attempt to answer. She was sitting, mouth open, watching the television, nodding appreciatively. Only her fingers worked, apparently independent of her mind, increasing the endless scarf.

"Was it ... did you know someone called Morgan? Jenny Morgan?" Vicky asked.

She was astonished at the effect of this name. For the first time since they'd entered the room, the old lady turned to look at her.

"Ivy Morgan's girl?" she said. The knitting needles stopped.

"Did you know her?" Vicky urged.

"Ivy Morgan's girl? 'Course I knew her. Knew her since she was born. Ivy and my Joan, they were at school together, weren't they?"

"Could you ... please, could you tell me about her?"

"Ivy Morgan? A year or two younger than my Joan ..."

"Not Ivy. About Jenny."

"What's it all to do with you?" the old lady asked.

"I think ... I think she might be a sort of relation of mine," Vicky said.

"You don't look like her. Pretty little thing she was. Ivy used to bring her over to see me. Nice manners she had, too."

"Does Ivy ... her mother, still live here?"

"Moved away, she did. She and Tom. Couldn't stand to be here any longer after it happened."

"After what happened?"

"After she died, of course. Their girl. Didn't you know that?" the old lady said, with satisfaction of giving bad news.

Vicky couldn't speak.

The knitting needles clicked again. Mrs. Godfrey's eyes went back to the television. As far as she was concerned, all the excitement Vicky could provide was now over.

"Do you know where her mother went to? After Jenny Morgan died?" But Vicky couldn't understand. Ivy Morgan? Tom? Hadn't her mother said she hadn't any family?

"No I don't. Never comes to see me, that I do know, though I'm told she's been more than once to see to the grave."

"The grave?"

"Told you she'd died, didn't I? Her grave. The girl's grave."

"Jenny Morgan's? You mean ... She's buried here?" It didn't make sense.

"Where else would she be buried? Now you be getting

along. You've made me miss the best part of my programme with all those questions. You can see yourself out," Mrs. Godfrey said, her eyes fixed unwaveringly on the television, her expression showing that she didn't mean to answer any more questions. As Vicky went towards the door, however, she called out, "Mind you close the front door properly."

Vicky did let herself out. She walked through the sunny garden and out on to the road. Through the village, towards the church on the further side. She could see its squat grey tower rising above the small, misshapen trees that bordered the road. The burial ground would be round that church. But it didn't make sense. How could her mother, who had died in a London hospital, whose relatives had never come forward to claim her, be lying here?

As she went through the lych-gate, the clock on the tower struck the half hour. Half past four. She'd have trouble getting back to Lodenek. But she couldn't worry about that now. First, she must find her mother's grave.

16

On the Tuesday morning Price woke up in his small, shabby room in Bodmin, to the sight of another brilliant, blue day. He ate a greasy breakfast, but before going the next fifteen miles to Lodenek direct, he drove up a short way on to the moor. Seen in sunlight, it had lost all the menace it had held the evening before; it was now impressively beautiful. Price left the car and walked out on the side of a hill, purple with heather, droning with bees. He could smell the honey. He walked for more than an hour. Rough going, but it was good to have something different from pavements to tread. There were acres of bracken, still green, broken here and there by sheep tracks. And everywhere there were the huge blocks of stone, sometimes erupting from the ground as if they'd been pushing their way upwards for a thousand years, sometimes stacked, like the building materials of a giant, making shelters, great unearthly cairns, terraces, towers. It was a world Price didn't often manage to look at simply to enjoy. He took deep lungfuls of the clear air, listened to larks trilling high above him, and was pleased he'd come here for this, if for nothing else. After he'd returned to his car, he drove slowly till he reached a wayside inn, where he found a surprising lunch of home-made pie, good bread, excellent cheese and real beer. He'd been ravenous, and after eating he felt a new man.

He drove to Lodenek, and, perhaps again to put off the moment of confrontation, down into the old town. He liked it, in spite of the throng of tourists. He liked the old houses clustered round the quays. He liked the rapidly widening stretch of bright water in the estuary. He'd have liked it a lot better, he decided, out of season, a small fishing town, getting on with its own business of living and trading, surrounded by, and depending largely on, the sea.

He drank another beer – not as good as the one he'd had on the edge of the moor – and sat for another twenty minutes on one of the stone mushrooms by the side of the quay. Then he retrieved his car from the car park and started off up hill towards St. Riok.

It was just after three o'clock.

He drove slowly, looking about him as he went. There were plenty of cars on the road, family cars, most of them. He saw small heads bobbing about against the rear windows of the cars that passed him. Sometimes an open two seater containing a windblown young man and his girl careered past – too fast, said his policeman's mind. There were several pedestrians. Again, family parties, mostly, the occasional hiker with a back-pack bowing his shoulders. As he passed side turnings off to coves and beaches, there were Mums with pushchairs and dragging kids. He didn't notice or recognize the back of a solitary girl in a pink print dress and shoulder-length dark hair.

On the outskirts of St. Riok he saw the little police station and stopped. He went in and found a sleepy middle-aged constable, reading the *Western Morning News*. Introduced himself and asked politely for the information he'd come to gather.

Constable Williams had lived in St. Riok for the last ten years. Before that he'd been working in Truro, so there was a lot of earlier village history he didn't know at first hand. Penrose was a good Cornish name, he agreed, but he didn't know of any Penroses living in the village since he'd been there. But Hele, now. There was a sight of Heles living in Lodenek, and over to Trelore there were four or five more. Grandfather Hele had married for the third time in his seventies and there'd been another young family. The older children hadn't been too pleased about that.

116

There was no Mrs. Hele in St. Riok right now. There might have been seventeen years ago, he wouldn't know. He wouldn't know where she might have gone either, but he reckoned it wouldn't be far. Mrs. Roberts might know. She was the Vicar's wife and she'd been here twenty years or more. The Vicarage was on through the village, opposite the church.

Mrs. Mary Yelland?

This evoked a different reaction. Constable Williams knew Mrs. Yelland. Of course he did. Had seen her nearly every day when she'd lived in the village. The school-mistress she'd been. Before his time, but he reckoned everyone in St. Riok knew Mrs. Yelland and she knew everyone. She must've taught just about everyone living round these parts. She wasn't living here in the village any longer. Five years ago she'd gone to live at the Mare Sands. A house her doctor son bought for her, where he came down to with his youngsters for the holidays. About three or four miles away. You took the road to Northsea and turned off to the right after passing the church.

"Is it an official enquiry, sir?" he asked, ready to set the machine in motion if the answer was yes. Price said, no. It was a personal matter. A friend of his had mentioned that he thought he might have relatives living in these parts, and as he happened to be in the neighbourhood, he thought he might as well ask around.

Before he left, he threw another name at the constable.

"Ever hear of anyone called Morgan living round here?"

Constable Williams shook his head. No one of that name in the village now. He reckoned, though, that there might have been at some time. There was a farm along the road that people sometimes called "Morgan's", its real name being Penstemon Farm. But the family living there now were the Rogerses. If there'd ever been any Morgans around here, they'd gone.

Price thanked him, and went out to sit in his car and con-sider what he'd heard, and what he should do next. He could go to Trelore and chase up the Heles living there. It was a smallish place, wouldn't take him long. Or he could call on the vicar's wife and find out what she could tell him. On the whole, he thought his best course would be to go direct to see Mrs. Yelland. She had been the one to report the disappearance of the missing girl, and she might put a quick end to his search by telling him that Helen Penrose had to her knowledge not been pregnant when she'd left, or that she had turned up again later, at a date which would prove she couldn't have been Vicky's mother. In any case he couldn't think of a better source of information about a village than the schoolmistress. As the Constable had said, she must have known everybody, either through their kids or when they were kids themselves.

The grey church tower stood out plain against the cloudless blue of the sky. Price drove towards it. A grey stone wall on his right outlined the churchyard and beyond he could see a signpost with its arm pointing down a road which must be the one leading to the Mare Sands. The road was narrow and twisting and he was driving very slowly. Which was how it happened that he saw the girl standing under the roof of the church's lych-gate. Standing quite still, staring out into the road. He slowed down still more, his instinct for trouble telling him that she was unnaturally still. To his total astonishment, he recognized her. It was Vicky.

17

Price stopped the car, got out and went across the road. He saw that Vicky was in a state of shock. He wasn't sure that she'd recognized him.

"Vicky? What's the trouble?" He imagined the worst. She had heard some part of her mother's story which had knocked her off balance for the moment.

She stared at him without answering. He touched her on the shoulder and said, "Vicky?"

In a voice he wouldn't have known as hers, she said, "Why are you here?"

He tried to speak naturally. "Got a few days off. I'm just driving around, seeing different places."

She still looked dazed. He said, "You on holiday here too?"

She nodded.

"Are you with Chris and your Dad?" He'd have found Chris's straightforward approach reassuring just now.

"They're in Lodenek. We came over in the coach." She looked at the clock face on the tower. She said, "Dad'll be mad at me."

He didn't understand. But the first thing was to get that stricken look off her face. He said gently. 'Something's upset you, Vicky. Tell me."

She said, "It's that I don't understand. My mother . . ."

"You've seen someone who's told you something about her?"

"I saw the old lady. The one who knitted the shawls . . ."

119

It meant nothing to him, but he knew better than to inter-rupt.

"She said my mother was dead. She said ..." She was shivering.

"Try to tell me."

"She said she was buried here."

"*Here?*"

"It's true. She is. Over there." She pointed to the far side of the small enclosed churchyard.

"Show me," Price said.

She led the way. They went on the path round the side of the church, passing the ancient graves of people long since dead. Tall, massive head-stones, with moss and lichen growing over the deeply engraved names. Graves of whole families, the occasional heavy stone mausoleum. Vicky turned off the path now, and threaded her way between the grassy mounds, towards a corner where the monuments were more modern: smaller but not less ornate. Under a marble canopy a marble angel read a marble book. Some of the mounds were decorated by flowers.

Vicky pointed. At the head of a grave where the grass grew long, was a Cornish cross of granite. Price bent to read the name.

JENNY MORGAN
BELOVED ONLY DAUGHTER OF IVY AND THOMAS MORGAN

"That's her," he heard Vicky breathe.

Price pushed back the grassy leaves and stems that covered the lower part of the plinth. He said, "Vicky! Look!"

They read together,

DROWNED WHILE TRYING TO SAVE ANOTHER
AGED FOURTEEN.
THE MAID IS NOT DEAD BUT SLEEPETH

The date was nineteen years old.

"She died before you were born," Price said.

"Then how ...? Then she wasn't ... She wasn't my mother."

120

Price said, "You told me your mother . . . Mrs. Stanford . . . didn't think Jenny Morgan was her real name."

"There could have been two people called that."

Price thought quickly. He said, "Vicky, if your mother did come from somewhere round here, she may have known this girl. They'd have been about the same age. When she wanted a name that wasn't her own, she might have borrowed one. She'd have known that . . . this poor child wouldn't have minded. Couldn't be hurt." This was not the moment to tell her about his own line on the girl who had gone missing from the village.

Vicky sighed deeply. She stood up. Price took her by the elbow. As they walked back towards the road, he realized that they had been in the part of the burial ground reserved for children. Some of the grassy mounds were pathetically short.

He led her out to his car and opened the door for her to get in. He said, "You need tea. We'll find somewhere."

"The coach goes at half-five. I mustn't be late," she said.

"What coach? I thought you said your father and Chris were in Lodenek?"

"We're just over for the day. We're staying in Falmouth. I've got to get back."

"I'll get you there in time. Don't worry." He drew up outside a terrible concrete caff and ordered two cups of tea. He and Vicky sat at a rickety, none too clean table, and he saw with relief that she began to look more like herself.

"What brought you here, to St. Riok?" he asked when he thought she was ready to answer questions.

She explained about the shawl. The pattern of knitting which no one else knew. She told him how it had been chance that she'd seen the shawl on the other side of the county. She didn't have to explain how she and her Dad and Chris happened to be in Cornwall in the first place. He could guess how that had come about.

He asked, "Does Chris know all this?"

"She knows about the shawl. And she knew why I wanted to come to Cornwall. Because of what that woman said. About my mother being Cornish. Perhaps."

121

He said abruptly, "We'd better be getting along." He didn't want her to begin asking him any awkward questions. She'd had enough shocks for today. She wasn't going to hear the names Yelland, Hele, Helen Penrose from him until he knew what there was to know about them. That meant that she was going back to Falmouth feeling that the whole expedition had been a failure. She hadn't learned a thing. Poor kid! She must have built her hopes high after that unlikely discovery of the shawl pattern, but all she had found was a ghost. The spectre of a little girl drowned in these treacherous Cornish seas long ago.

But supposing he discovered something that would be comforting and not disturbing? Because he was not abandoning his own private search now. If there were people she should meet, a story she should hear, it must be now. He said, "How long are you staying in Falmouth?"

"Only till Saturday."

Price said, in what he felt was a heavy, almost official tone, "I might call in and see you if I'm over that way before you leave . . ." He thought she sounded unduly grateful. He was uneasy. But then he reflected that she'd been through a lot that afternoon. Not only that, but he'd got her out of a pickle by giving her this lift back to Lodenek. She'd never have been there in time for the coach at half-five unless some other driver had taken pity on her.

He wanted to keep things cool. He said, "I don't know where I'm heading for yet. Might not get as far south as Falmouth."

She said, "It's not that far."

"Well. If I'm around tomorrow or the next day, I'll drop in. Better let me have your address."

He fished his notebook out of the car's door pocket. He hated himself for behaving so much like the policeman he was. While he drove down the hill towards the little harbour, Vicky wrote down her Falmouth address. He drew up at the bottom of the hill, just out of sight of the harbour and the car park.

"You get out here, Vicky. Then you won't have to

explain to your Dad why you accepted a lift from a stranger in a car."

He'd meant to make her laugh. Instead, after she'd got out, after thanking him with her usual careful politeness, she said suddenly, "But you're not a stranger." Then coloured brilliantly and walked away.

He watched her round the corner towards the coach terminus, still with that feeling that there was something he didn't understand, hadn't quite caught up with. Then he reversed neatly into a side street and swung up the hill again. He was going to find out for himself what Mrs. Yelland knew about Helen Penrose.

18

The road to the Mare Sands turned off, as Constable Williams had said, just beyond the church, then wound about, past a farm, a duckpond, then a space of fields and hedges, another farm, and now the villas and bungalows began to stand closer together. The road turned sharply to the left and Price found himself by an open grassy space in the middle of which stood a telephone kiosk. On the further side of the space was a shop. Over the door he read that Arthur Phillips was licensed to sell tobacco, and that this shop also housed the post office.

There were plenty of customers inside. Price waited his turn, and when the customer before him had loaded up two bursting carrier bags, he asked the man behind the counter, "Does Mrs. Yelland live here?"

The man leaned his comfortable stomach against the counter, prepared for conversation. "She do. Down to the Sands. Tretheways, the house is." He jerked his thumb. "Last house before where the cars is all parked. Can't miss it."

Price thanked him and turned towards the door, but the man was not going to miss an opportunity for gossip. "You were at school to her? Over in St. Riok?"

"Who, me? No, I wasn't," Price said.

"Thought you might have been. Hardly a day in the summer when one of them don't turn up here. Hundreds she must've had through her hands in her time," the man said.

As he walked out to his car, Price wondered if Helen Penrose had been one of those hundreds.

He drove down the road in the direction of the jerked thumb. Downhill for half a mile. Through the open car window Price could hear the waves and smell the sea before he reached the open sandy space which was clearly the parking ground. Parents were packing their cars with weary, damp children, picnic baskets, wet swimwear, beachballs, all the accompaniments of a day on the shore. True enough, the house next to this space, looking towards the sand dunes which separated it from the beach, had its name Tretheways painted on the white gate. A pleasant, low-built house of whitewashed brick. Tamarisk, flowering in pale pink spires, waved above a stone wall guarding a small lawn, speckled with daisies.

Price opened the gate, went into the glass porch guarding the front door, where geraniums bloomed on wooden shelves. He rang the bell.

It was an impressive woman who opened the door. Old? Over sixty, perhaps more than seventy. Snow-white hair sprang vigorously from a high broad forehead, below which were lively eyes and an emphatic, but not dominating, nose. A good mouth, firm chin.

"Mrs. Yelland?" Price said.

She scrutinized him as she must have done other middle-aged men who called unannounced at her door, and who then proved to be little Eddies, Robbies, Tommies to whom she had taught the alphabet and their tables, years before.

"You don't know me. Detective Chief Superintendent Price."

She said instantly, "Police? There's been an accident?"

"Nothing like that. It's a . . . a personal matter."

She considered him gravely. She asked, "Personal to you or to me?" He liked that. He liked her quickness and her quietness. A woman who wouldn't panic easily.

"I have a friend who thinks she may have relatives living in this part of the country. Or may have lived here some time ago. I happened to be driving round here, so I asked and was told that you used to be the schoolmistress in St.

Riok. I reckoned you must have known a great many of the local people." Not exactly nothing-but-the-truth, but that could come later.

She smiled. "I've certainly known most of the last two or three generations in St. Riok." She held the door a little wider. "Won't you come in? Then you can tell me the names."

He thanked her and followed her into a sitting room with a long window looking towards the sand dunes. There were shelves of books. There were dozens of framed school photographs. Ranks of small children were lined up on the walls, staring solemnly – for a school photograph is not an occasion for levity – down at Price and Mrs. Yelland, facing each other in the room below.

She sat quite still on an upright wing chair. She said, "Yes?"

He plunged directly in. "Did you know a girl called Helen Penrose?"

She said eagerly, leaning forward, "Helen! What happened to her? You know her?"

He must not prolong hope. He said, "No, I don't know her myself. I'm not even sure that she's still alive. But I need to know something about her."

"Is this a police investigation?" she countered.

"Not officially."

"What is it, then, Superintendent?" She had great dignity. He saw that she was distressed. He knew he was on delicate ground.

"I think I'd better tell you the whole story."

"Please do."

He left Vicky out of it. He told her that a girl, giving what was thought to be a false name, had died in a London hospital over sixteen years ago. That he'd had the idea of looking up the file on girls missing around that time, that he'd been helped by a report that she had a West Country accent, that the name of Helen Penrose had come up. That although the trail was old, he'd thought it worth while to try to see if it was the right one.

"When he came to the end of the story, there was a short

126

silence. Then Mrs. Yelland asked, "She's dead?"

"If the girl I'm looking for was Helen Penrose, yes. I'm afraid so."

She said, "I've often wondered. I couldn't believe she wouldn't have let me know what had happened if she'd been alive."

Price said, "I understand it was you who reported her missing? Not the aunt she was living with."

"Yes, it was me. I knew her very well. Better than Doris Hele – that was her aunt."

"Could you tell me something about her? Helen?"

"She wasn't born here. Did you know that?"

"I don't know anything about her. Only that you reported her disappearance to the police."

"She lived with her aunt. That was after her parents died. It was a road accident, they were all three killed, Helen's father and mother and the baby. Helen was seven. There weren't any other relatives, only Doris. She was Helen's father's sister."

"Where had she been living before her parents died?"

"They lived in Bristol. Her father was an engineer. He worked in one of the big motor works there."

"How did it turn out, her coming to live in St. Riok? Did she and the aunt get on with each other?"

Mrs. Yelland said emphatically, "No!" Then she said, "It wasn't all Doris's fault. She had her own worries. Children of her own, and a husband who wasn't much good to her. Having to take Helen in must have seemed like the last straw. I think she tried. But Helen . . . she'd come from a city. She'd been almost an only child. There'd been books in her home, her mother had time to talk to her. You'd be surprised what a difference that can make to a child." She mused.

"She came to your school?" Price prompted her.

"She was a very bright child. She didn't fit into the Hele family. I was sorry for her. I used to have her round to my place so she could read and talk. She's been used to having a lot of attention from her mother, and she missed her . . . painfully. She used to borrow books from me and then

127

come back to talk about them." She smiled at the recollection. "I suppose she was the sort of pupil every teacher dreams about. She really wanted to learn."

"When she left your school, where did she go?"

"The Raybridge Secondary."

"Was she still there when she disappeared?"

"No. She'd taken a typing course and she had a job in Northsea. It was called a secretarial job, but I think she was really just a junior typist. I know she had to make endless cups of tea. A waste. I'd wanted her to go to college. She had the brains. But it wasn't possible. It was the money. It always is." She paused, then said, "I'd have helped if I could. But my own boy was at medical school then, and it was as much as I could manage to get him through. I lost my husband in the war, you see." She looked at Price, defying pity.

"How long had Helen been in this job before she disappeared?" It was a key question. He tried to keep his voice level. She hesitated before she answered.

"You'll think it very peculiar, Superintendent, but I'm not quite sure."

"Could you explain?"

"I didn't see so much of Helen after she'd started working. She had to leave early in the morning and she didn't get back till late. Late for a village, that is. Sometimes I wouldn't see her for a couple of weeks, and then it would be at the weekend. I was busy too. And . . . I don't know if you'll understand this. I felt so close to Helen, I was so confident in her, that if she didn't come round for a time, I didn't worry. I knew that when she did, we'd always be on the same terms. Does that sound very stupid?"

"I think you and she were lucky," Price said.

"Yes. We were."

"So when did you begin to worry?" Price asked.

"I think it must have been in the summer. Late summer. I'd been away visiting relatives after the term ended, then when I came back I realized that I hadn't seen Helen for a month. No, months. I went round to see Doris to ask after her." She stopped.

"What did she say?"

"I blame myself for this."

"For what?"

"I should have seen she was lying. She said Helen had gone to stay with friends."

"How did you discover that it wasn't true?" Price asked.

"When I went back, a few weeks later to ask for Helen's address, she was confused. She contradicted herself. I told her I didn't believe her. Then she told me that Helen had gone."

"Did she say when? The date?"

"She said it was June or July. But I think she was covering up. I think Helen had been gone before that."

"Do you remember when you saw her last?" Price asked.

"I tried to think, after I'd heard Doris's story. I couldn't be sure. I knew I'd seen her in the Easter holidays, but after that . . . no. I didn't know. I blame myself for that too."

"How was it, then, that no one reported her missing till the December?" Price was as gentle as he could be.

"You're right, I did everything wrong. When I heard that Helen had gone without leaving a note, nothing, I asked Doris what she'd done about it. She said that at first she'd believed Helen was stopping with friends in Northsea. She did sometimes stay overnight with a girl she'd met in the office. But never more than a night at a time. I told Doris she should have reported Helen as missing . . ."

"She could have had an accident! She could have been drowned!" Price exclaimed, thinking of Jenny Morgan.

"That's what I said. 'Aren't you worried?' I said. So she said, of course she'd told the police. A week after Helen had gone, she said."

"That wasn't true, either?"

"I didn't know that then. I should have guessed. You'll think I didn't care," the old woman said.

"I'm sure you cared. Sometimes it's difficult to know what to do for the best. So you discovered that she hadn't made the report?" Price said.

"I went to see Mr. Lewis. He was our local Sergeant. He'd never heard a word about Helen's going."

129

"And this was, when? Which month?"

"The end of November, I think. It might have been right at the beginning of December."

"Did you tell Helen's aunt what you'd done?"

"I think she was relieved, really. She knew that she ought to have done it herself. I could have forgiven her putting it off like that. At first I think she really did believe there'd be a letter or a message or something. It wasn't as if they'd ever been close, and she wasn't what I'd call an organized woman. But I couldn't forgive the lies. I can't forgive myself for believing them, either. I was selfish. Too much wrapped up in my own problems."

"Perhaps you expected to hear from Helen too?" Price suggested.

"Yes, I did. I couldn't understand why she hadn't told me what was in her mind."

She'd been hurt, Price thought. She must have felt that she'd given a lot and been poorly repaid by this lack of confidence. He could imagine the mixture of wounded feelings, pride, delicacy and anxiety which would account for how she'd behaved.

"After you'd reported Helen missing, did you hear anything of her?" Price asked.

Mrs. Yelland shook her head. "They said I mustn't expect too much. They told me how many young girls go missing each year. It made my heart go cold. I used to think, 'Suppose it had been my daughter?' It was terrible knowing that Helen was one of those – those lost girls."

Price asked, "I suppose you haven't a picture of Helen?"

"Of course I have. I have pictures of all my children." She rose slowly and took one of the framed photographs from its place on the wall. She held it towards Price. Two rows of staring young faces, stocky little bodies. In the middle of the front row, a younger Mrs. Yelland, distinctly recognizable. She pointed. "That's Helen. She would have been about ten."

The child Vicky looked out at him. Where the enlargement had distorted, this tiny reproduction showed the dark fringe of eyelashes, the rather prominent cheekbones, the delicate, bony nose. Very dark hair falling to well below the shoulders.

The likeness was enough to convince him. He felt the sweat break out on his neck and forehead.

"Is this . . . relative . . . at all like Helen?" Mrs. Yelland was asking.

"Very much." He couldn't, for the moment, answer more.

"You said that Helen died. In a hospital. What happened?"

Again he knew that he must choose his words carefully. He said, "Do you know if she had any boy friends? Or one in particular?"

He hadn't reckoned on the quickness of her perceptions. Her hand went up to her mouth in the age-old gesture of distress. She said, "You mean, she had a baby?"

"Yes."

"Please. . . ?"

"She had the baby in a London hospital and she died two days later. No one knew who she was or where she'd come from. She didn't give her own name . . ."

She interrupted him. "What happened to the baby?" She was trembling.

"The baby lived. It's because of her I've come to see you," Price said.

"What is it to do with you? Why have the police. . . ? Who are you?" the old woman cried out.

Price said, as gently as he could, "It's nothing to do with the police. I told you, I'm here on holiday. It's a personal matter. It was pure chance that I got to know this girl . . . your Helen's daughter. She's a schoolgirl. She's sixteen. Lives in London. She's a very nice, intelligent girl. Like her mother, I'd guess." He saw that Mrs. Yelland was still agitated, and he went on speaking, to give her time to recover. "When her real mother died, she was adopted by a woman who'd had her own baby in the same hospital at the same time. She brought both the girls up as her own. No one could have been a better mother. I think your Helen's daughter has had a very happy childhood. But the mother

131

... the adopting mother ... died earlier this year. Now this girl wants to know something about her real parents. It's difficult, because no one could trace any relatives, and your Helen hadn't talked about her background. She was only in the hospital for a very short time before she died."

"You said she didn't give her real name."

"She called herself Jenny Morgan," Price said.

"Jenny? But Jenny was drowned," Mrs. Yelland said.

"I discovered that this afternoon. I found Vicky in the St. Riok churchyard, looking at her grave. She didn't understand . . ."

"Vicky? Who is Vicky?" Mrs. Yelland asked. She was trembling again.

"Vicky is the girl we're speaking about. Helen Penrose's daughter."

"What is her real name?" He thought for a moment that she would faint.

"Stanford. That's the name of her adopting parents . . ."

She shook her head. "No. Vicky. Is that her real name? Who gave it to her? What is it short for?"

Price said slowly, "I'm afraid I don't know. It's what she's always been called. Short for Victoria, I suppose. I've always assumed it was the name her real mother gave her." Victoria didn't seem a likely name for Mrs. Stanford to have chosen.

There was a silence. Then Mrs. Yelland said. "You said she was here? In St. Riok?"

"She was there today. But only for a few hours. She came over by coach from Falmouth. She's staying there with her father and her sister."

"I should like to see her," Mrs. Yelland said.

Price hesitated. He said, "She's ... sensitive," and thought how inadequate this description was. How could he convey, to someone who had never met her, Vicky's capacity for hurt? Her quivering awareness of atmosphere? He said soberly, "I'm anxious she shouldn't be too upset. I know that whatever she finds out about her mother's background may be disturbing, and though I see she has a right to know . . ."

132

Mrs. Yelland said, "I don't think I have anything to say that would disturb her. I was very fond of Helen."

"Perhaps you could tell her something about Helen's parents? Her grandparents?" Price said.

"I could tell her what Helen told me. Yes. I suppose I could tell . . . Vicky . . . about her grandparents."

"But you have no idea who her father might have been?" Price asked.

"Would it be possible for you to bring her to see me?" Mrs. Yelland asked, not answering this question.

Price did a quick calculation. It would probably be better for Vicky to hear what this woman could tell her than to continue to search on her own account. Or than to remain in ignorance and unsatisfied. He felt he could trust Mrs. Yelland. If Vicky was sensitive, so was she. He said, "I'll try to bring her over to see you. Not tomorrow. The day after. Would that be all right for you?"

She thanked him. Said, "Do you mind if I don't see you out?" He left her sitting in her chair and went out of the house, and over the sand dunes on to the now empty beach. He walked down to the sea's edge, where small waves sucked and moulded ripples in the pale sand. In the valleys between the tiny ridges, were tiny shells. Behind him the long marram grass waved and whispered in the light wind. It was cooling down, the sun approaching the wide rim of the horizon. Price thought with apprehension of the meeting he must supervise in two days' time. He didn't want Vicky to be hurt. He wished he could keep her from being hurt ever.

He remembered Jill Peabody. She was right. You couldn't protect people from hurt, however much you tried, however much you loved them. It had been right to agree to bring Vicky over. He would call on the Stanford family tomorrow evening and make arrangements for the following day. Meanwhile he still had to find somewhere to spend the night. A thin wind from the sea fluttered his shirt. He shivered, and returned to his car.

19

On the Thursday the weather had changed. No more hot sun. No blue sky. A wild west wind drove a curtain of rain across the Falmouth bay and tore at hedges and trees on exposed high ground.

"Shame the weather's broken," Price said to Vicky, sitting very quiet beside him.

"I like the wind," she answered.

He drove for another five miles without speaking. He was trying to think how to prepare her. The trouble was that he didn't know for what. When he'd arrived at Mrs. Rodd's boarding house the evening before, he'd explained briefly to Mr. Stanford and Chris that he'd met Vicky by chance near Lodenek on Tuesday and that today he wanted to take her to meet someone he thought might interest her. A real Cornish character, a retired village schoolmistress. It sounded a bit lame and he was surprised that Mr. Stanford appeared to accept it without question. All he said was, "I suppose you'll want to go with the Superintendent, Vicky?" She'd said, "Yes", and that had been the end of the conversation.

This morning, once they were in the car, Price asked, "What did you tell your Dad last night after I'd called, Vicky?"

"I told him all about Tuesday. Chris thought it'd be better."

"So he guessed that we're going to see someone who knew your mother?"

She nodded.

"Did he take it all right?"

"He wasn't as upset as I thought. He wasn't hardly upset at all."

"That must have made you feel better," Price asked.

She didn't answer. He took a quick look sideways and said, "Didn't it?"

"How do I know he doesn't mind because it doesn't matter what I do? To him."

Price said, with what sounded to him a sort of forced jollity, "Vicky, nonsense! Of course it matters. He's been your father all these years!"

"Sort of." Almost inaudibly from Vicky.

"Not sort of. You've been part of each other's lives. Of course he cares what happens. I know I would, if I'd been your father."

He wondered if he'd said the wrong thing. She turned towards him and said, on a choked breath, "If you'd been . . ."

He didn't want her getting too emotional. He said quickly, "I don't suppose I'd have done as good a job as your Dad."

"You would!" She was too emphatic. Damn it! And he hadn't begun to prepare her for what awaited them at the end of the journey. He said, "Vicky!"

"What?" She was startled by the change of tone.

"I just want you to think a bit about where we're going. This lady we're going to see. Mrs. Yelland. She knew your mother."

"What did she say about her?"

"She was very fond of her."

"She must have said more than just that."

"You can ask her yourself. That's why we're going," Price said.

After a moment's silence, Vicky said, "There's something else. Isn't there?"

"What do you mean?"

"It's not just Mrs. Yelland. Is there someone else there too, who knew my mother?"

135

"I didn't see anyone."

Vicky said, "Did she tell you anything about my father?"

He could say with truth, "No, nothing." But he had to go through with it now.

"Have you thought what you'd do if you ever did discover who he was?"

"If I just knew who he was? Nothing else?"

"Suppose you knew where he lived? What sort of job he had. If he was married. That sort of thing."

"You think Mrs. Yelland knows, don't you?"

"If she does, she didn't tell me."

"Will she tell me, do you think?"

"If she does, what will you do?"

There was a long silence. Price drove on, not glancing at his passenger. He could feel the tension beside him.

At last she said, "I just want to *know*. I don't want to upset anyone. Only . . ."

"Only what?"

"How do I know what I'll feel until I do know? If she tells me, I mean."

He drove on without saying any more.

He deliberately avoided going through St. Riok. He didn't want Vicky reminded again of the shock she'd had there. He approached the Mare Sands from the other side. They drove up and down small steep hills, along country roads, over bare downs where the twisted trees demonstrated the force of the prevailing wind. When they were high on the cliffs, the wind nudged Price's car across the road and they could hear the roar of the waves below, thrashing at the rocky shore. The rain had stopped, but the sky was sullen. It was quite unlike the gentle summer weather Price had seen here two days before.

He drove down the road to the house by the sands. When he pulled up, he looked at Vicky. She was very pale, but she smiled at him. He thought, "That's my girl!"

He rang the bell and almost immediately Mrs. Yelland opened it. She looked first at Price, then at his companion. She said, "This is Vicky?" her voice tight with control.

Vicky put out a polite hand. "How do you do?"

136

Mrs. Yelland took it. "Come in. I'll make some coffee."

They sat in the sitting room, dark now with the storm clouds racing overhead. Price looked from the old woman to the girl, each waiting, each taut. Vicky drank coffee, nibbled a biscuit. Mrs. Yelland sat upright in her winged chair. She said directly to Vicky, "The Superintendent has told you I knew your mother? I was very fond of her. She was . . ." She sought for the right words. "She was a good girl."

The old-fashioned phrase hung in the silence. Outside the waves bombarded the shore. Vicky bent her head.

As if she'd been briefed, the old woman went on from there. She told Vicky all she knew about the family. The home in Bristol where Helen had spent her first seven years, the accident, the death of both parents, the move to St. Riok and the aunt who hadn't time or money enough to be kind. She drew a picture of a girl growing up in alien surroundings, a girl who had responded to the comfort of understanding and encouragement that her schoolmistress had been able to give. Above all she made it clear that she had liked Helen. Just as he had come to this tame conclusion, Price heard her say, "I couldn't have loved her more if she'd been my own daughter."

Vicky said, "My Mum . . . that was my adopted Mum . . . she said she was a lovely girl."

"Your Mum was right."

A pause. Then Vicky pulled out of her pocket the faded snapshot she'd shown Price on her visit to Scotland Yard.

"I found this in with the papers my Mum kept. The adoption papers and things. – I don't know if she knew who it was. None of us did."

Mrs. Yelland took the snapshot and glanced at it. She said, "Yes." It was clear to Price that it wasn't new to her. She had no need to study it closely.

"Do you know who it is?" Vicky asked.

"Yes. I do know."

"Is it my father?"

The old woman looked at Vicky, a long enquiring look. Then she said, "Yes, it's your father. Quite a long time ago,

137

when he was a student. I didn't know that Helen had this..." She checked herself. Then handed the photograph back to Vicky. "You'll want to keep this."

Vicky took it in silence. When at last she spoke again, she said, "My Mum said . . ."

"What did she say?"

"She thought probably my father . . . my real father . . . didn't know about me. She thought my mother might not have told him she was going to have a baby."

"I'm sure she was right about that too. I wish I'd known your Mum."

"She thought my mother wouldn't have wanted to make him feel as if he ought to marry her. She thought he probably couldn't have."

"Your mother . . . Helen . . . was a very loving girl. She was independent, too. She'd learned to be. She'd had quite a hard time. If the boy wasn't in a position to marry, then Helen would have been quite capable of thinking that she'd spare him the knowledge. She'd have believed she could bring up a child by herself."

"My Mum said that my mother must have loved my father. A lot, she said."

Price held his breath. Did they know what they were saying? He heard the old woman say, "Vicky, I'm sure she did. And I'm sure he loved her too."

There was a sudden flurry outside the window. A child, a boy of about seven, had run into the garden and was knocking on the long window. He was calling out, "Gran! Gran! Let me in!"

Mrs. Yelland started out of her chair. She went to the window. Price saw that her legs were shaking so that it was difficult for her to walk. She opened the window and the boy tumbled in. The wind tore in with him and the framed photographs trembled on the walls. She shut the window quickly.

"Jacky! How . . . Are you all here?"

"We've come early to give you a surprise," the boy said.

"Where's your Dad? He's here too?"

"He's somewhere. Outside."

"We ought to be going," Price said, standing up. Vicky followed his example. He saw that, for the first time in their short acquaintance, Mrs. Yelland was at a loss.

"I wasn't expecting my son and his family till the weekend . . ." she said.

"We'll take ourselves off, then. Thank you so much for your help." He would have liked to thank her, too, for the manner of her help, but there were things you didn't say.

She shook hands with him. She held out a hand to Vicky, who took it silently.

"Come and see me again. One day," the old lady said.

"I'd like to," Vicky said.

A woman now appeared in the doorway. She was small, well built, fair, pretty. She greeted Mrs. Yelland "I hope you'll forgive us descending on you like this, Gran . . ." then stopped, seeing the two strangers in the room.

"Of course, Pam. You know you can always come without letting me know. My visitors are just going. This is Mr. Price. He's a friend of a relation of one of my old pupils. A very dear pupil." She smiled at Vicky, a slightly shaky smile. Turning to the woman in the doorway, who had said, politely, but without much interest, "How do you do?" to Price, Mrs. Yelland asked. "Where's . . .?"

The woman said, "Victor's outside, unpacking the car. We've brought . . ." She stood aside to let Price and Vicky pass her, and as they went along the passage leading to the front door, they lost the end of the sentence. A moment later they were outside the house, in the tearing wind.

Just beyond the garden gate a tiny girl was skipping around a man who was unpacking the loaded boot of his parked car. He looked up as they passed and gave them the countryman's courteous, "Good day!" He was tall, like his mother, big-boned, with an attractively intelligent, ridged face. Price gave him his "Good day" back. Vicky said nothing. The tiny girl hid behind her father's legs, peeping at the strangers, making it impossible for him to move. He took her by her fair waving hair and pretended to pull. She shrieked with laughter and clung the tighter. It was clearly a long-established game.

Price felt Vicky hesitate. His heart sank. But before he'd had time to formulate a thought, she had moved on again. They got into his car, he reversed and drove out of the car park and up the hill. Vicky did not once look back.

Price drove for nearly a quarter of an hour in silence. Then he said, "Bad luck, her son and his family arriving just then."

"Yes." But after a minute, she said, "No. I'm glad I saw him."

"And her. The old lady."

"I liked her a lot," Vicky said.

Another pause.

"She really did like my mother, didn't she?"

"I'd say she loved her," Price made himself say.

He drove on. He knew that Vicky was crying, though silently. Once or twice she rubbed her hand across her eyes. Price sat beside her without speaking, apparently concentrated on the car and the road. He was surprised at his own turmoil. All his years in the Force should have accustomed him to dealing with distress, he'd seen enough. But he was feeling again, with that unexpected passion, that he didn't want Vicky to be hurt. He rehearsed in his mind possible things to say which would comfort or calm her, but nothing seemed right.

Presently he drew up outside a pub he'd marked down on the outward journey. He said, "Let's get a bite to eat, shall we? I could do with half a pint and a sandwich, couldn't you?" Get some food into her, he thought, before she goes back to confront Mr. Stanford and Chris.

Too cold to sit outside, and he couldn't take her in. He said, "You stay here in the car. I'll fetch us something." She nodded, without speaking, and he went off to the bar to see what they had to offer. Not much choice. He carried back two plates of sandwiches, beer for himself, cider for Vicky. She looked at the food doubtfully, but he was pleased to see that after a slow start, she ate as if she'd discovered a hunger she hadn't recognized. Once she was properly started, Price kept the conversation impersonal. He asked her about Falmouth, what she and Chris had done there,

140

what they'd seen. Half an hour later she was answering his questions normally and looking less strained.

When they were back in the car, driving along the last stretch of road through dreary Penryn, down the hill to the Falmouth docks, she asked suddenly, "When are you going back to London?"

"I'll start back this afternoon. Stay somewhere on the way tonight."

"Then it wasn't just for a holiday, you came here?"

He remembered too late his excuse for being in St. Riox. He said, "I just had a few days off," but he knew this wouldn't satisfy her.

"You came down here to see her. Mrs. Yelland," she said.

It seemed best to say, "That's right."

"How did you know about her? You didn't know about the shawl . . ."

He explained. His idea about missing girls. The clue she had supplied that her mother might have come from Cornwall. How Danny had come up with the reports from the seventeen-year-old file. "I was feeling fed up with London and the heat. It was an excuse, really, to come down here. You know, a policeman doesn't like to make a wasted journey, even when he's on holiday."

She wasn't amused. She said, "I never thought you'd do that. When you said you'd help. It's . . . wonderful of you."

"Stupendous?" he said, teasing.

She said, impatiently, "That's . . . I mean. I don't know how to say it . . ." Her voice was full of tears. Warning bells rang in Price's head. Plenty of silly women had thought, because he'd helped them, that they felt something for him which he certainly didn't feel for them. Now Vicky. He realized, too, that this wasn't just another silly girl whom he could brush off, politely but firmly. It was Vicky, his brave girl. Of course she was het up, emotional, probably didn't know, herself, what she was feeling. She'd had quite a day. She'd been introduced for the first time to the whole story – or as much as she was ever going to hear –

141

of her dead mother. She had seen the man who was almost certainly her father. She must have had to give up a hundred young fantasies in the moment when she had walked past him outside his mother's house, and had allowed him to remain a stranger. After an experience like that, it wasn't for him to tell her that whatever dreams she was cherishing about him could never be translated into waking reality.

He astonished himself by his own reaction to this, which was an angry denial of the impossibility. Vicky wanted him to tell her that his journey down to St. Riok hadn't been just the instinct of a policeman on the scent of a mystery, nor a convenient whim. She wanted him to say that he had undertaken it for her. He had an impulse which horrified him by its urgency, to tell her that this was true. He wanted to stop the car, to put an arm round her and to comfort her, to feel that he could be the father she'd given up, as well as something else, which she might not yet have thought of. In the split second which is all the imagination needs to encompass a lifetime, he saw Vicky holding a baby in her arms, her face alight with the knowledge that she had come full circle, to be part of a family that couldn't be more her own.

She was sixteen, and he was forty-eight.

Vicky was surprised by the sudden acceleration of the car, but the Detective Chief Superintendent's voice seemed no different from usual as he said, "It was a loose end that hadn't ever got tied up. Policemen don't like loose ends, you know. It makes me feel a lot better now we've got it all sorted out."

That wasn't right, either. It sounded like a deliberate snub. He added, "You know I'm pleased to have been able to help you. I've never forgotten how you and Stephen Rawlinson helped me with that Wilmington case."

"We couldn't not have. The baby . . ."

He had nearly said, "And that poor girl . . ." thinking of the stolen baby's mother. But that was too near the bone. He said instead, "Do you see Stephen ever nowadays?"

"Sometimes I do." She didn't sound very enthusiastic.

142

That awareness of each other which Price had noticed during the time of the Wilmington kidnapping must have died away. On Vicky's side, anyway. Another twist of the heart, but he meant to keep his head. He said evenly, "I liked Stephen. A nice boy."

"It was him suggested I came to see you in April," Vicky said.

Irony! There were several comments Price could have made, but all he said was, "I'm glad he did."

"I'm glad too."

Time to be entirely practical. "Vicky, you'll have to direct me now. Once I get into this town, I lose all sense of direction. Got lost three times trying to find your house yesterday."

She gave him clear, composed instructions. Ten minutes later he drew up outside Mrs. Rodd's front door. Geraniums climbed round it, profusely blossomed, as roses grow in harsher climates.

"Won't you come in?" Vicky said, not moving from the passenger seat.

"I won't, if you don't mind. I'd like to get at least halfway to London before it gets dark."

She got out of the car and stood, awkwardly, on the pavement, holding the car door.

"Bye!" he said, to help her.

"Bye! And . . . Thank you for . . everything." But she still didn't close the door.

"Have a good time tomorrow for the last day of your holiday," he said.

"I suppose . . . I shan't see you again?" she said, not looking at him.

His hand went out towards the ignition key to stop the engine. He wanted, as he hadn't wanted anything for years, to say, "Get back in, Vicky, we've got to talk." But he left the engine turning over and he forced himself to say, as casually as he could, "Of course you will. I'll come round to see you in London one of these days. We'll keep in touch."

Just what they wouldn't do. Ever. She gave him a tremulous sort of smile then, and shut the door. Price drove away along the little street, forcing his mind forwards to reality, his immediate future. He would concentrate on the work waiting for him in London, absorbing, demanding. That should satisfy him. He thought also of Jill Peabody. She would be waiting for him too. Dependable, Jill, a good girl. The phrase echoed Mrs. Yelland's summing up of the girl she had loved like a daughter and wrenched something inside him. But he drove on, and he too, did not look back.

20

Chris and Mr. Stanford were out when Vicky went into the house, and she was grateful. They might not have asked her anything, but she would have felt their unspoken questions pressing on her mind, and her mind felt bruised, tender, needing undisturbed time.

The sky had cleared and the wind on this south coast was nothing like as tempestuous as in the North. She couldn't stay indoors. She went down the hill to the small beach where she and Chris had swum. Empty, only a few cars parked at the head of the cove, with the occupants sitting glumly behind their windscreens, reading papers. She walked along the beach barefoot and looked at the endless sea, stretching away in tumbling grey water. It was like her mind, restless and turbulent, saying the same thing over and over again. She didn't formulate what it said. She knew that she wished she could have been beside the sea on the other coast. She thought, "That was where I began. I belong there." But then she knew that wasn't right. Part of her belonged there. Now that she knew it, she had somehow to fit it into the rest of her living.

When she got back to Mrs. Rodd's, Chris and her Dad were there.

Mr. Stanford said, at once, "Vicky? What happened?"

"There was a lady. She knew my mother."

"Go on."

She had wept silently in the car, but now, trying to repeat

145

what Mrs. Yelland had told her, she was choked by tears. She could not get out a whole sentence. Chris came to sit by her, an arm round her. With uncharacteristic patience, Mr. Stanford waited to hear.

"Is that all?" he said, when she had managed to give most of the story.

"She said . . . she'd liked my mother a lot." She couldn't say the word "love".

"She didn't tell you anything about . . . who your father was?" Mr. Stanford asked, and Vicky, aware of an unexpected tension in his voice, said, "She just said she was sure Mum was right. About them having loved each other."

There was a short silence. Vicky wiped her eyes.

"You feel better now?" Mr. Stanford asked.

Vicky nodded.

"You don't want to go off asking any more?"

"No, Dad."

"If the weather clears up tomorrow, Chris and I thought we might take the trip to the Lizard. All day. Only if the sea goes down, though. I'm not going on one of those herring boxes if there's waves like we've seen today," Mr. Stanford said.

"The waves over at the Mare Sands are huge. Much bigger than here," Vicky said.

"Big enough for me this side. You don't see them like that at Bognor," Mr. Stanford said.

When they were in bed that night, Chris said, "Won't you really go on looking any more?"

"I don't think so."

"Dad'll be pleased if you don't."

"It isn't anything to do with Mum. Really, Chris."

"I know that now. But Dad . . . he's been jumpy all day."

"Dad's never jumpy."

"He was today. I think he got really worried."

Vicky had something to say that was difficult. But she owed it to Chris to try. "You know, finding out about my mother. I mean really, not just what she was called, but

146

what she was like. It doesn't mean I don't think just as much of Mum. Our Mum. I think it makes me feel... More..." She couldn't quite finish.

"Does it? I'm glad. " After a moment, Chris said, "I don't think it was just because of her."

"What wasn't?"

"I think Dad thought if you found out about your father, you . . . you wouldn't sort of care about him any more."

In Vicky's ears she heard Price's, "Of course he cares what happens." In her mind's eye, she saw the face of the tall man outside his mother's house. A stranger's face. She said, "I do care. A lot. But I can't tell him."

"You don't have to. He'll know," Chris said, with that certainty which Vicky sometimes so much envied.

"Chris!"

"What?"

"If Dad asks, you might tell him."

"He won't. But if he does, I will."

Back in London, while the endless hot summer dragged on, Vicky found herself bored and impatient. A disagreeable combination, and not what she'd expected. She had thought that once she'd found what she'd been searching for, she would feel at peace, as if a hunger inside her had been satisfied. But the peace she'd hoped for seemed more like emptiness, as if all her energy and will had drained away. She felt as if she had spent most of her life up till now searching for a secret, something that was going to make sense of all the contradictions, the inexplicable fears and longings that made her sometimes one sort of person, sometimes another. Now the secret was out, and she didn't feel any different, only flat and miserable.

She had a summer job in a small shop which called itself a boutique. She helped to sell trendy clothes to girls of her own age. It wasn't interesting enough to engage her attention. She did it for the money, and at the end of the week she hadn't the energy to spend what she'd earned. Everything seemed to contribute to her feeling of living in a waste land. Nothing to look forward to, nothing to plan. Sometimes she felt as if the only thing that made her life worth while was her world of fantasy. She imagined herself going again to Scotland Yard to see Superintendent Price. Sometimes, in her fantasies, he came to see her. Sometimes he said outright that he wished she had been his daughter. He had almost said as much when they'd been driving across Cornwall. He had gone all the way down there, just to help her. He must like her quite a lot.

She imagined herself going back to visit Mrs. Yelland. She would hear a great deal more, there, about her mother, and perhaps about her father too. But she knew she wouldn't go yet; she needed time before she would be ready to take on the relationship which might be waiting for her down there, in that house by the shore with its pounding seas.

Depression accumulated around her like layers of grey fog, curtaining her off from the real world and from feeling strongly about anything. She seemed to be living like an automaton. She was still in this state of mind on an evening at the end of August, when, coming out of the boutique after a busy and sweltering day, she found Stephen on the pavement, waiting for her.

"Vicky!" He wasn't sure what reception he'd get. He hadn't seen her for ages, hadn't tried. She'd been cool, the last time they'd met. He hurried to say, "I wanted to tell you. I've passed! My 'A's. Heard this afternoon, and I wanted you to know at once."

She managed to say, "That's great! Congratulations!" With a decent show of enthusiasm. Enough to encourage Stephen to say, "Come and have a drink to celebrate before you go home?"

She hesitated, then said, "All right. Thanks."

"There's a pub in the next street. You can sit outside. A sort of garden." The pavements were busy with people pushing to get home after a day's work. Stephen said, "I suppose you haven't heard your results yet?" but they were shouldered apart before she could reply. When they were within talking distance again, Vicky said, "Another two weeks to wait. That's what they said."

148

They reached a side street. Vicky asked, "How did you know where I was working?"

"I saw Chris." He didn't add that he'd gone round to the house especially for that purpose. He asked, "Has she decided what she's going to do next term?"

"She is going to the Tech."

"And you?"

"I expect I'll stay on and do my 'A's."

"You'll go to University?" Stephen asked.

"If my 'A's are good enough."

"What'll you read there?"

She didn't have to answer immediately. They had reached the pub. It stood back from the road, behind a small courtyard where little trees grew in tubs, and a trellis overhead supported a flourishing, though grapeless, vine. Vicky sat in one of the white ornamental ironwork chairs, while Stephen went off to the bar. She watched the other people drifting in and thought, "The Detective Chief Superintendent is right. He's nice really. I do like him quite a lot."

"It's a ginger beer shandy. Hope that's all right?" Stephen said, putting two tall glasses on the unsteady little iron table.

"Lovely. Mmm! It's beautifully cold," Vicky said, taking her first long delicious gulp.

"It must be hot in that shop where you work," Stephen said.

"It's like hell. How I imagine hell, anyway. Terribly hot, and full of stupid girls getting stuck in pants that are too tight for them."

Stephen laughed. "How much longer are you working there?"

"September. Beginning of term."

"You didn't tell me what you're taking for your 'A's."

"I'd meant to take English. It's much my best subject. Only now I'm not sure."

"Why?"

She was embarrassed as she said, "I'm not sure how much use it'd be. I thought perhaps if I got through the 'O'

149

level science, I might do biology and chemistry. And physics, if I could manage the maths."

"You mean, you'd read science?"

Looking into her shandy, Vicky said, "I don't suppose I'd ever get into medical school?"

For a wild moment, Stephen thought this might be something to do with his choice of career. But it couldn't be that. He said, "You've changed your mind, then?"

Vicky didn't answer that direct. She looked round the little enclosed yard and said, "It's nice here."

"What made you think about doing medicine?" Stephen asked again.

Apparently irrelevantly, she said, "I went to Cornwall."

Stephen, alert, asked, "You found out something about your mother?"

"Yes."

He said, "Tell me," not knowing if this was the right invitation. But after a moment she began. At first it was in unconnected sentences, which he found difficult to follow, then gradually in longer and more coherent passages of narrative. At points in the story he had the courage to interrupt.

"No. I don't understand. There was a real Jenny Morgan, then? Why did your mother take her name?"

"Because she was dead. Long before my mother left St. Riok. The old lady ... Mrs. Yelland ... thought it might have been because they'd been friends. Because she knew Jenny wouldn't have minded. Lending a name."

"I still don't understand how you got to see this Mrs. Yelland. Was it because of the other old lady? The one who knitted?"

"It was the Superintendent. You know. It was you told me to go and see him. In the spring."

"How did he find out about her?"

"He got someone to look up missing people. Then when I'd told him my mother was Cornish, they got her name and the place she'd come from."

"And he told you about the old lady?" Stephen asked.

"He went down to Cornwall to see her."

"Just for that? You mean he went all that way just to see her?" Stephen felt something that was remarkably like jealousy. Then he saw how ridiculous this was. The Superintendent must be fifty, or nearly. He'd probably been down in the West Country on a routine enquiry anyway.

"He said he was on holiday," Vicky said, looking into her glass.

"Have another?" Stephen said.

"I shouldn't . . ."

"You must need it after spending a day in hell."

"All right. Thanks."

It took him longer, this time, to bring the full glasses back to their table. "Bar's filling up."

"Almost worth my terrible day," Vicky said, sipping.

"Vicky!"

"What?"

"You haven't said anything about your father. Your real father. Did you find out anything about him?"

"Yes."

Stephen said, disappointed, "You don't want to tell me."

She said slowly, "I'm not sure. I think I might. Only not now."

He kept his eyes on her face. "Was it . . . bad for you? Upsetting?"

"Sort of. Yes."

"I suppose now you feel sort of let down?"

This time she looked back at him. "How did you know?"

"Well. You know. If you've been thinking about something for ages, and trying to do something about it, and then it happens . . . it's over. There isn't anything left to make an effort for. I generally feel like that after I've got my exam results. Tomorrow I'll probably feel terrible. Miserable. As if I'd come to the end of the world."

"That's right."

"I felt like that after we'd found that baby. As if nothing exciting was ever going to happen to me again."

"I suppose I did too," Vicky said, thinking how much had happened in the past year.

"Have you still got your piece of the Egg?" Stephen dared to ask.

"Yes. Somewhere." She sounded casual, but really she knew exactly where it was. Lying in her box, biding its time. She didn't quite trust it, even now. She said, "Do you want it? I'll give it back if you do. It's silly, keeping it separate from the other bits."

"No. Don't. It isn't as if the Egg was all there, even with your bit, anyway. Don't you remember? When we tried putting it together, it wouldn't hold. There's still something missing."

"It's a pity you'll never have it all in one piece again," Vicky said.

"I don't know. It's only a puzzle. It doesn't matter."

"I'll tell you what!" Vicky said suddenly.

"What?"

"If I gave you my bit and we put it together, like you did that day after we'd found the baby, we might be able to see what was missing and we could make another. A bit that fitted in, so it would be a whole egg again. Couldn't we?" She was animated by the idea.

Stephen looked at her across the rickety little table. She was flushed now, and eager. He said, "Yes. I'd like to try."